Seventh Ratica

Seventh Ratica

Mike Gutowski

Christine Filippou

Mike Gutowski

Seventh Ratica
Ω
a
Mike Gutowski
novella
"It's raining. Come on in.
So, it is. Come on out."

"The mind is its own place, and in itself can make a heaven of hell, a hell of heaven." -- John Milton, Paradise Lost

---

Ratica: writing material of the ancients, i.e., what they write on, such as skins or parchments.

Here Lays A Birth

What's built on a lie crumbles on a lie. Some mistakes can be forgiven but never become forgotten. She never told him "I love you". So, there existed in fact a limit to her cruelty evidenced by this singular lie she could not allow pursed from lips sweet. Perhaps her humanoid male connections to date had not survived those of the brutish persona status, or the infectious narcissists of which legions of their armies trolled the social connection plains. To exist in the mind and or body of either sex involved much trouble and toil emotional. After a certain age it started to feel like death chased after you.

I suppose there existed a script for living life, but as scripts are wanting to do, they become edited at the corners, in the scene descriptions, amidst the verbiage of characters in long and wide swaths sometimes, and in tiny little marks of rejection or correction. Here I present the script, changes and all for this life, for your perusal, and final say. Furk it all thoughts served as the mind's refresh key swirly. Somewhere out there, amidst strange shades of black and white, existence resided. Find it. Grasp it. Live it. Grope it. Die it. Okay, enough self-pity. Get on with it. Why must the "it" be such a marvelous mystery? Taxing, it is. Waxing not marvelous, too. Contemplation sometimes sucked. In dream state especially.

Okay. So, they killed me. The malcontents. The greedy. Still, my mission beckons. And free food awaits, edible unguilty in the digestive phase, like that time a friend didn't really want to spend with me, yet did, and I tried to not gorge on their polite patience during the time ticks and clicks of vociferous drudgery spits in the process. Processing thoughts ground away endless, even if only over the course of seconds, it seemed in the effect.

So, they think I'm dead, the humanoid perpetrators do. Traitors they are anyway. Dispense with them I will. Dispense. Then completed mission awaits, then rest. Sweet rest. The sugar syruped donuts fresh and warm and sweet of smell like a dew spun morn. This death in me changes the mind thought formations. Muffled voiced vocabulary. Confused. Sound mulled, molded as rubbery goo. At least thoughts of the first kill to come has aroused energy in me. Which one.

The closest. Time to sniff it out, the humanoid target chosen by the wind, the sand grains disturbed, the turning worms ahead. My underground vision serves well in this need time. Underground thinking is the worst. Too many distractions of dirt, varied sun-fearing critters like moles, shrews, ants mark trail moments.

Much too much turf navigation involved. The busiest of busy above ground humanoid streets and avenues treaded desolate compared to down here where life clings madly to every cold grain of soil.

Above ground travel, in walks beamed as a much easier course traversal. Eyes open, usually a path already carved by humanoids long ago as the tried-and-true motion tool prevailed. Underground remained slower and more deliberate, but to avoid the directional encumbrances of above ground paths served as advantage. Underground allowed creation of multiple short cuts. Just had to watch out for tree roots, rocks, and underground humanoid implants like cables, sewage pipes, gas lines. The latter named not necessary entanglements in this desolate place given prior humanoid influences resided near nil in effect.

And varied gray lines snaked along and under the land's topside, persisted random. Ancient pre-humanoid existence marks, perhaps. Vagaries of focus misery at best. What are they for? Mysteries created by the humanoids for who knows what. Not in the public literature. Or perhaps planted deep under the soil by other dimension beings and not yet discovered and included in the terrestrial history. Vagaries. And varied.

The unknown presides disgusting deep. Disgusting of the kind difficult to see for mapping a path, or after mapping to follow it, or during following, to traverse it safely, and the worst scenario, reach outward to the ending point and find not what's expected whether in a bad way, disappointment, or in a good way, beyond wildest dreams. Either way, a painful longing or remembrance cloaks the mind in the mental prison brick built strong as conclusion for the journey. Remembrance stings, one way or another.

Going underground moaned danger. A temptation to stay pulled strong, as if gravitation pressures increased. There existed so much more life in that place, below ground, rich full of minerals, stones, gems, littlest of creatures eating, procreating, silent screaming life's sounds and vibrations. Cruel too. No morality. Life exploded random of pattern or purpose. Biology's satyr of torture and death, death, death. Destroyed to build. Built to destroy. Almost infinite repetitive until from the unknown place of no thought or reason, popped forth another biological entity somehow produced out of the messy mix of chemistry cooking. Secret evolutions of dirty work, humanoids be damned. They're more microbe than humanoid. Bacterial cell battles raged like an apocalypse inside, outside and all around the body polite. Mated for better or worse.

Humanoids believed if there be just one thing that could be figured out, they would gain complete control of all existence. Know everything. Understand everything, but perspective points biased the view. Not true. Never true. Tens of trillions of things are yet to be figured out. Tens upon tens of trillions of circumstances are yet to have been calculated. Control is a fiction only followed by humanoids. Lesser creatures only attempted control of the immediate surroundings, then adapt to changes encountered thereafter. To know of the past ruled as the key to understanding a future, but much of the past remained a mystery. Just discovering revelations of the past could take millions of years, yet time didn't necessarily consider such an effort doable. Time swatted efforts like flies.

The wind didn't care. The sun didn't care. Nor did the land care. The weather scoffed at it all. Fictional cultures and clans thereof tied themselves up amongst each other for help, support. Made sense to a point. Except the nature of humanoids repeated the same emotional refrain of complete control and obedience to the summoners. Nature didn't care. No machine extant or hypothesized controlled the caged gods. Fictions in the head suffered stings and bruises of cruel intellect masters.

Ghoul clans had figured out such life configurations eons ago. Their inner voices allowed self-reflection, internal conversation, self-observation. Also, realized fools rejected wisdom outside their programmed comfort zones. Thanks, media. Thanks, religions. Thanks, politicians. Rulers all know the stupid and uninformed or misinformed existed far easier to control after eons of washed brains. Thanks, educrats. Simple respect of each other, for each other, remained a most difficult of learned lessons to perfect, mysteries mysterious, served as directions given for all destinations. Less perfection, less direction. Step upon step of knowledge accumulation and practice of healthy habits did not remain mysteries to even biological creature specks, yet the most sentient of all, the humanoids, remained chained to the mousetraps of their own intellectual devious inventions.

Simpler constructed living creatures shared a common language worldwide in the howl, growl, whimper, simper, purr, whir and basic facial attributes mimicked or displayed. Scents served specific purpose, used air current avenues to communicate mood and want. No gods intervened or stirred the pot merry or wild in these brains. Sniffs, licks, grunts and kicks served enough as language means.

Humanoids, imbued with the same instincts, further invented hundreds of languages as if purposeful in an attempt at ultimate confusion.

Time wasting seemed their best honed skill. Breath energy exerted in the wilds served purpose at every passed moment. Humanoid breaths continued, throughout evolution, to include increased number of contemplation moments so much so that physical inactivity became a pastime. The results generated more entertainers and less innovators, until a critical chasm grew large enough to become noticed. Notice served existed in now time. Plenty of time to figure out what steps necessary can be accomplished to reverse course and find another road, to what destination uncertain.

Meanwhile, a smoke, a toke, a half-cocked choke served to pass the time away. Controls of nature took a back seat in the vehicles of entertainment drivers. Work, work, work, sleep. Work, work, fun, sleep. Work, fun, fun, sleep. Here the tipping point sketched out a reach. Hang on. Anything could happen next. In the spun, a seed of greed had begun sprout, infection spread like a disease hidden, but one day, stretched long and strong across the breach of boredom time, ready to continue the species evolution in further directions mysterious either evil or fruitful intentions. And even fruit rotted, so no guarantees resided steady in such cycles.

Reboot

He focused again his eyes as the floor scale flooded calculations unmarked, yet destined to gleam the weight of its occupant. Him. No patience meant no matter. He stepped off. Anyway, the scale number curiosity only arose after a straight but wiggly toilet piss, from a standing position. Echoes of the sound still rung round in his ear cavities. Maybe next time he could move the scale just next to the toilet, stand on the scale, then piss into the toilet. That effort would confuse the flat-assed little metal bugger.

His mind groaned like an empty stomach in need of more sleep solitudes. Still sleeping, maybe, I am. "I don't trust you much, little bugger. And I trust myself even less."

All of nature mocked humanoids as if to say, "you are not part of this". All of time laughed out loud at humanoids because they resided as slaves of universe vagaries. Lived moments morphed into memories of varied and gray emotional degrees fast, slow, disappeared.

Lived moments died fast. Some memories just didn't want to hold on. Some didn't deserve the attention of another moment's grasp. Letting go seemed a whole world unto itself, threaded seams struggling towards murky freedoms.

Time for cleaning squeezed a nick out of brain cells. Brushed away the murk slog, then pinched at nerves. Go for it. Get it done. Another day teetered on the brink of lost or won.

Moments ugly tweaked naught but mastication's, masturbations, tergiversations from pleasant to perverse. His urge to slap away such thoughts dueled for attention. Task lists flittered like mosquitos buzzing worries into ear canals. Bite worries. More nicks. End already, this moment, he desired. Ends never cleared. Beginnings beckoned unholy. A perfection sought distraction from such acute cranial stresses even tuned tortures taut. An imperfect road surface these mind travels exposed.

Awake. Asleep. Mid wake. Mid dream. Always the same dreary stream flowed in sound and fury hums. Reverberations endless. No echoes if he was lucky. Echoes served loneliness punches. Microscope or telescope. See deep. See far. All the same in the end game. All the same.

"That's what I'm here for. Eat, bleat, and excrete." A smirk put an unvoiced, yet poignant explanation point upon this humanoid wisdom existence exhortation.

"What? No sexual duplicity?"

"Not necessarily necessary, like dairy."

"Furk. That's new-born calf wise."

"Yup. Tip that cup."

Time steels all. What goes down must come up. The weather doesn't care what you think. Direct reflections of the most common humanoid trait of falsehood. Such a trait existed as a fantastical club all to itself. We lie, to ourselves, every hour of every day, even while sleeping. We accuse others of being deceivers, but we are guilty of the same or similar weakness of cerebral spine. The weather just doesn't care.

"J'accuse!"

"Talking to yourself again?"

"What do you think?"

"Why?"

"Because I don't want to continue the group articulation of lies to get along, to socialize."

"The most important thing to learn in living of one's life is that lies exist in the environment of humanoids, in numbers greater than roaches and rats combined."

"Disgusting vous."

"Who?"

"You!"

"That's a rather pessimistic view of life."

"Yes, it is. It lives. For me, pessimism lives as true feeling; as defense to virus spread lies."

"People are more forgiving of their own errors than they accord to others who abide, hide among alike flaws."

"Errors of a kind flock together, you mean."

"It is the eros of lies."

"Wingless. Droll."

"Perhaps one day it shall break the moon, this rock flock."

"Just another day of traveling among many places and ending at the starting point."

"No wiser, in the end."

"We've all got skin in the game."

"Lies are needed to grease the survival wheels."

"To help society in function, if not in form."

"Some would call it calculated courtesy."

"Or roars amidst sores."

"I calculate your courtesy."

A mutual and repetitive, instinctual bow occurred as their spines permitted. Then nature pissed from the heavens and the dance started all over again, until many others joined into a silent step somber serenade of humanoid to and froe, here, there everywhere, into the cosmos dim, hiding a grin, universally so, amidst raindrop toots low. Alive of thought. Dead of deed. Such and such, so and so tugged at a bend of the reed. Time passed lost. Repetition grinded out an accordion's wake into the tune of Dett's "In The Bottoms/Barcarolle/Morning".

"Geppetto, where art thou?"

Most probably, carving the wood. If no ejaculation has yet to raise an ugly spray, then the chance has been missed, slid away. Chance is everything and all, from Winter to Fall. How much arrogance does it take for to believe a god or one of the god minions came over to talk with you about something so special, no one else on the whole planet deserved a presence in the conversation?

"Well, the world is full of sickos, psychos, sycophants, and serial killers."

"Good furking point."

"Right. You are the specialist of special humanoids. Only you can help me to carry out the grand plan."

"Which means the 'you' is the most skilled liar, cheat, and passive aggressive in the history of the universe."

"Sounds so political in nature."

"Bingo!"

"Bongo!"

"Burpee!"

"Boffo!"

"Now you must bow and obey me because god says so!"

"The litany of punishment methods from banishment to death and every method in between stands well known, historically."

"By god, we killed that conversation topic."

"Furking yes!"

Sounds of nature began to intercede upon, tickle, their inner eerie ear cavities. The planning significant. The adventure implementation easy.

"Eerie is the night of sounds unholy."

"Let our molded moldy brains have a go at it."

The last day beckoned for all living things at any given moment. A shallow deceit of thought helped to mask such inevitability, because stale comfort of the more sentient life forms required it. Every humanoid required sustenance of some sort. Planned a future uncertain, for the hell of it, for the succor of it, why not. Micro-organisms would survive, at least, to evolve, expand in scope, until sentient beings, for better or worse, might crawl towards the top of the food chain again, and morph into whatever the food chain permitted. It seemed all magic beans and random waves, or winds, depending on the habitability landscape or spacescape.

Aurie's first path always flowed through a dark forest of jutted sharp twigs and tree branches unholy, bent on beating back the very being of the noble author trekker. Cuts, scrapes, punctures to body and soul parts inevitable befell the walker, regardless of dress material protective efforts.

Gradually, the first destination point beckoned in the form of a bridge. Appropriate words poked a need to join the ideas together. Smooth the trodden intellectual seed patch path a bit. Truth served merely as a means from point A to point B, never mind the C, yet it hovered in the shadows and transformed in revelatory presentation at planetoid motion whims. There goes the light, and so too a clear sight. In this world there is no time for guilt.

Whatever resided as tenant under the wooden and moss

carpet laden bridge braced by iron brackets, in the way of danger or death, either enhanced by height or fall depth into whatever indecipherable horrors could be imagined, such as ravaging ice-cold waters run wild, or sharp and skin piercing instrument, or bone shattering rocks and boulders perceived, beckoned as a further observation test mettle. The more likely a decision to continue to move forward presented itself, the less likely the answer could become "proceed" in the traveler's mind. To traverse the bridge which expanded outward from the lonely side to the aloneness other side destination became a jagged decision wall. No clever shortcut or dubious heroic transformation presented itself as a true travel or transgression method option.

"That is one large engorgement of thought," he spoke quietly to himself, so as not to alarm the tiny, hidden stalkers of the wood. Need to remember. Add this rumination tickle to the Ratica parchments. "Perhaps the ancients will forgive me should I forget."

Many blood coveters of insect and arachnid variety craftily followed or had designed pre-planned necessary survival assaults along the traveler's path, of their own design necessity. These tiny creatures had no choice, for to not collect victims and blood drain them meant near or eventual death potential at any moment. The traveler began to realize such biological mechanisms were at play on his path. His body simultaneously served as food supplier or murder demon for all creature species within reach or vicinity of his physical presence. He was merely a carbon copy of sustenance needs; a walking fruit; a stumbling animate carcass, and nothing more or less for the forest creatures. And they were of the same category as him, from a perspective point. Amidst such woodland beauty lay death silent, creeping around, up, and down, along, and beside.

Bumps and bruises along the way beckoned, for all concerned. Scabbed wounds became worn like clothing. Healing might occur along the way, physically, yet mental damages remained for burial either immediate or at point of eventuality in order to continue the just one more blistered, then calloused step to intellectual revelation. He dragged too many moments of regret around within him so that some of his steps forward seemed an impossible task. Mistakes of moment, errant choices, horrid failures left his psyche battered soft, pliable.

Psychological repair lay hopeless upon his mental plain. He long ago sorted and boxed them and the lessons otherwise learned from these events he necessarily recalled in dream states. He had yet to complete his many repeated attempts to successfully reach the other side of the bridge. He began to wonder if his efforts were meant to fail. What a completed crossing would mean still eluded his conscience.

Every humanoid is born of free will. It's just a matter of whether they wish to exercise it, and more particularly, while other humanoids squeeze out attempts to exorcise it. Choice becomes whether to cede the gift away into the ether of beyond.

We're all liars. Some of us just consider ourselves more noble liars than others. That bland bite of an intellectual pestilence stings sore. If you chain yourself to someone else's opinion, then you're neither free nor intelligent, enough. There's always hope, if blessed with enough time. Time steals all.

It works for now. Acts as a more palatable think than it works fornever. Nothing works forever except for the universe engine. At least we tell ourselves such in order to ingest just one more breathe of hope; exhale one more steam of search, like shedding work clothes for comfort threads.

The body attached to the genitalia stands irrelevant as long as the body is clean, inside and outside. Rake up the leaves from my lawn and the neighbor's. After all, the tree on my landscape excreted the leaves forth in a natural blanket spread unnatural by the winds which suffered the want of chaos. All have heart heat and soul. It's just a matter of whether the mind will lead. That was a mindset milkshake drop. The straw nearly broke from exerted sucking power. Poky wonderland.

He needed to escape the sounds. Even the billboards and ads thereupon created a mind noise. Fight the man. Fight the power. What's with the "fight for it" syndrome. Marketers, social organizations, politicians regularly claimed a fight existed. Perhaps in their own minds, but their purpose seemed to cloud the minds around them to make it easier, more convenient to seize control. Exercise dominion over listeners.

Why did humanoids seem convinced they had to fight for anything and everything. Work for it sure. But working isn't fighting. Plan for it sure. But planning isn't fighting. The word choice served as intention to treat the mind as a chaos system, unorganized, dangerous. So, listen to the elite who know all, but want to know specifically none of their biological earth mates considered not of the class of preferred humanoids. Such is the cure recommended by commercial marketers. Doctors of the mind they pose ideas that need revolution, re-evaluation, reckoning of odd sorts. Choose a side or become crushed in the stampede. Fear of rejection swings as sword. A dark, dusty dawn always awaited.

Oh, I know. The marketing commercials foisted against the greater populace serve like magic tricks, spells, potions of deceit mechanisms. Corporate executives want everyone to believe they are fighting for it, no matter what it is. Such tactics unholy. And the way to win is to purchase the marketed solutions and escape the chaos of life, if even for a moment. Lipstick to pretty the facial expression. Hair styles to perk up the motion of emotion. Clothing under and over the body to enhance the visual humanoid form. And the politicians love the chaos. The calamity of life means the more the better for those humanoids in control of it all. The noise and clash of the system reverberates so loud and long in the minds of the consumers and workers. He enjoyed silence. Craved it. But here, no silence. Noise. Always noise.

If humanoids knew half as much about the brain thoughts and recollections recorded therein of their acquaintances, friends, and partners as they did about body parts intimately, the resultant horror mental injection would wipe out the extant population over time. Crushed the humanoid instinct for socialization would become. Many times, ugly minds created an impotence unevaluable. At least, the author of the following tale had considered such a termination.

But all things were never settled, as in the case of these matters at hand, still at long in reach, but in hand none the less. The rain started. Tap. Tap, tap. Tap, tap, tap. Taptaptaptaptap.

His look through the dress store's display window glass served as follicle screen. His eyes continued to focus on the threaded mannequins, their posture of tall and straight. Their slight flare of forehead, arms, hand fingers, and some of the faux humanoid structures even extended below the waist if not mounted sooner by white plastic boxes, as if the body type represented a grand trophy of stature perfection. Clothed all in varied cloth and color, they enticed an onlookers visual acuity and mental intensity, but after too long a gaze, their visions became a glaze, then a haze, and finally transformed into a reflection of the gazer. The author tried to refocus his vision, but a slight and subtle motion he spotted on the exterior of the window glass. He squinted at it, refocused his vision using the mind dial of his brain, then noticed across this unbusy and near devoid of humanoid activity an apparent living mannequin, clothed in a dark hood which connected to a cloth jacket and extended downward meshed fuzzy into similar color and cloth of pants. The shoes which seemed glued to the cement sidewalk betrayed slight of size feet hidden inside, or so his imagination told him.

The gazer across the street, she, seemed to be looking at him, he thought. Why? To test his perception of this moment, he moved his arms out a bit as if to allow them to seek muscle stimulation as alleviation to the stiff feelings cluttered in the body by lack of movement. His eyes noted the hooded figure's face move back and forth in a sideways motion, as if following his arm movements.

By chance each of them had become together entranced by the shop window display. A coincidence even if unusual in time complexity and duplicity. Her reflection showed a mimic of his arm motions. A new spark of thoughts injected into his mind by such actions evolved into so many thoughts he lost clear sight of her intent.

When he refocused his vision, she was gone. His eyes only, he moved, or darted, from side to side along the glass window display pane as no further movement of his body became considered necessary, so as to avoid suspicions of the sidewalk gazer. He judged her to be out of his sight range, but how swiftly she had accomplished such a feat puzzled him.

He considered himself an expert at interpreting moment motion complexity, but he couldn't explain what just happened, or the specific meaning of it, at the place behind him on the other side of the street. He refocused his vision back towards the mannequins although he had yet to move his head even a spec of distance towards or away from the display window glass. Their plastic gazes towards him still gleamed dead of meaning but the lips of each seemed to betray just a bit of a smirk undetectable or untranslatable to him in the moments earlier. Their narcissistic gazes still looked a bit too distant of emotion. Plastic has none, emotion. Art has not emotion. Interpretation of the vision brings forth, then unleashes the art gazer's inner mental machinations as means to connect with the inner thoughts and feelings of the artist. Whether a relationship born solely of intertwined minds develops, sometimes it existed too early to detect. He filed away such thoughts for further mental research times. He turned his body in the direction of the walking path along the storefront. A shadow movement attracted attention to him from the corner of his eye. He declined to look at the shadow directly. The mystery of it he preferred, at least for now, he'd throw these thoughts away to simmer a bit in the back of his mind. That's the excuse, for now.

A simple reader warning. Given my biological origin, I sometimes refer to myself as I, me, and sometimes as he, while my mind tries to find a comfort place to exist in the moment. Apologies. "He" means distant. "I" means closer present. A slim difference, but slim is where relevant margins exist. And me refers to a prayer state of mind. For instance, a prayer that latches upon any given moment of any given day, the Ghoul Orison.

Ghoul Orison

We exist within in a mental duality. There exists an I which displays itself to the outer world. There exists co-equally a "we" which displays itself only to the "I" secretly. A near constant struggle persists amongst and along the two-state boundary. This story attempts to exemplify the principle.

"What a world this place portrays. Humanoids and creatures destroy each other in so many ways. Ups and downs of prayers many and praise faint. No wonder the only remaining decision for the gods revolves around methods, means, and moments expended to raze.

Raze, raze upon the marbled steps of life's blight, of memories sewn tight into dawn's brightness assent. Raze then raise from darkness to light into darkness spent. Perhaps an experiment from beginning to end.

First life reigns, then death feigns another purpose. Rewards for these tasks cling as hopes upon many. Surely, a peace and calm reside in the next life aplenty."

Reminded myself, there existed a price to pay for the pursuit of any noble venture. Approach of morning harkens to the darkness of this day's mourning descent. Death of one portends life of another. A somber fade to black, then a virulent spritz of light.

"Still making friends with dream shadows?"

"Fiends, too."

"Figures."

"I only awaken to remember you."

"Always the fool."

"Never foolhardy."

"Dreamers do die."

"Or fade away."

"Die."

"Into the ether."

"That map is apparently lost in time."

"On the shelf. Right next to unhappy endings."

"What is a dream?"

"Past experiences interpreted. Present experiences defined. Future experiences anticipated."

"All nightmares, or fairy tales, or fruit cakes."

"Hocking. Always hocking your theories."

"A grand design."

"Illumination, even."

"That's the spirit."

"No, bird brain."

"Hawking, as in Stephen."

"A brilliant light."

Time for a mind brunch. Okay, now back to it.

"Oh, look at the time. My life is rushing away from me."

"Such is the universe, of sorts, out of sorts."

"Hungry now, thinking of torts, a rhyming word which reminds me of tortellini."

"The moon, a cheese, an object wronged by a random solar breeze."

"You and your lawyerly spaghetti."

"What specialty?"

"Real estate and land matters."

"Don't get him started on food nuances."

"Constitutional law."

"His next galaxy find. Looks like Tortellini."

"Constellations law be hammed."

"Eats better."

"Stuffed with a mix of meat, Parmigiano Reggiano cheese, egg and nutmeg and served in capon broth."

A low groan of a stomach solo began, then others joined in.

"Time to find that food galaxy."

"Wait. Did I hear a defamation of . . . of . . . what's the word?

"Character."

"No."

"Begins with a C?

"Wait a sec. It's coming to me."

"They check their watches."

"Corn crisps!"

"Funny."

"Not."

"Two words. Two syllables."

"Efficiency of thought, if not efficacy."

"I ate. I saw. I squandered."

"More like squatted."

Someone passes wind in a toot taut.

"Sweet."

"Wait. Not so much talking when we eat."

"Why?"

"Because it will take our minds off the primary purpose which is to enjoy the food sensations accorded towards our destination."

"These minds are serious land matters."

"More like dusty diatribes."

He didn't get out much. He waved his hand in the air just below his brow. Dust particles swirled and circled in the beams of dark sky ceiling light. Let their words dance. Silence be damned. Even if destiny dictated a different course. What group of we constituted we, he wondered. Get comfortable with yourself. One is the loneliest number. Still, it'll do.

Skin Tight

Time to pee again. Pee or perish. "Better to awaken, or I'll dream my life away." Alrighty, alrighty, alrighty, all right. Moments of failure, past failures, crept into his skull, both personal and social, as the jet stream of pee splashed deep into the toilet's humanoid-calculated abyss. In the sounds of splash, he summoned memories of days passed by, of no particular pattern, except by the design of his work plans, and moments of rest. Redundance sometimes portrayed a rhythm as cloak to imagined deceits. Too many notes of deeds future to tick off. Only the birds clicked sounds of sense. At least the thin, metallic-threaded screen window barrier muffled them enough to lessen drones of distinct clanged chatter.

"Really need to break these mind hackles."

Back to the couch. No accompaniment of toilet flush woosh. "I'll get it later." He rubbed his body and limbs along the cloth threads, burrowed in the entirety of his anatomy, found a comfort zone, then began the gradual dozy state needed for relaxation and recuperation. His mind continued the rubric of categorical construction required of this journey status. This body served him unwell in times of culinary digestion and waste expulsion.

He much preferred an elegance of Delalande's "Symphonies For The Kings Supper 6/Rondeau…". His imagination of the musical sounds helped pattern some pressure relief. A laxative the tones invoked. The point of everything is nothing and the nothing place is where it's at, if it can be found. Good luck.

Through the course of humanoid life, one cannot control the daily physical and mental encounters with others, which frankly change in intensity with age but eventually recedes into familiarity, lessens the burdens of understanding actions, as aging helps us to perceive the experience differently, due to familiar experiences repeated. He attempted to imagine the writing of his story notes into a manuscript readable by management Superiors.

"This fifth book, Seventh Ratica of calculation mine has

taken me to many places I've never imagined. Not sure where the words are coming from, or why, but write them I must, and do so, for me, and for you. I'm now finding it less difficult to find some gems during the word jumble dig. I suppose that is good for me. The first four book efforts involved much mental toil. The more times the journey is taken, the more familiar it becomes, seems. Much like job experience, there is training, then practice, then perfecting the skills learned and applied. Still not creating pastries on an assembly line but approaching such a possibility from a literary perspective.

Lucky enough to have lived a long time, it only takes the tapping of a few words on the keyboard to hear the musical emotion tones of a story, a character, a scene, then take those threads or shards of clay and form them into a beginning, middle and end, all set towards the goal of providing a beautiful and enticing journey for the reader, no matter the literary genre. I am merely a servant to the craft, as I now see it, but a willing one. I never understood why, but sometimes the why is less important than the 'do' of the what. I do it because I must. That simple it is, I guess. Each of you has similar experience in finding what you must do with your life."

He stopped his mental construction of the book. Awaited the mechanism of further inspiration. Attempted a return to sleep state. The door called.

"Knock, knock." The apartment front door clatter demanded his attention, loose hinges be damned.

"What the furk," he vaguely mouthed, not yet quite awake to give the vowel sounds their appropriate due. He reached for the Mountain Dew can nobly awaiting his attention, resting solemnly on the bedside table. Airy it felt, the can, upon his outstretched arm grasp, then hand and finger accompaniment squeeze around it. Tilted it towards his lips. Drops emerged only.

"What the furk." No symphony of taste played out for him, except scavenger drops as if the grub can had already been picked over for nourishment.

"Heck, only a few days rested there, on the side table. Only a few." He released the can from his hand for it to resolve itself a place on the hardwood floor, and moan metallic click sounds back to him as a retreat echo. Humidification beckoned lonely.

He raised his head from the sofa cushion in a quick spurt, riffed of cluttered mind like the bass solo of "Hot Razors In My Heart" by the rock band Crack The Sky, opened his eyes and noticed a white drywall ceiling above his head, farther away than his natural full arm extended reach. He looked at the hand connected to his extended upward arm. He wasn't sure if he recognized it. He shook his head to jar his eyes wide open, looked again, then notice a moving shadow enter his side glance.

A medium-sized cockroach skittered across the yellowed drywall surface, stopped as if waiting for traffic to cross the street, from a human perspective, then lurched forward in micro-fractions, antennae flittering into the air to measure safety issues.

He wondered what kind of bull hockey desired to raise an ugly head of mischief at the front door. Failed poets entered his head. Their authored words resided most famous in sentient stupid minds. His opinion, of no worth in the moment, served only as rejection selection to tease hate of the needed body motions of the moment's required response. A short walk would rid him of this humanoid motion curse.

Many physical motion types existed. Desired, undesired, adrenaline induced which fit the category of both, except only in extreme cases of dosage. The prelude to purgatory, as it were. Like it or not, it's a good moment, another moment, aches and pains serving as arbiter in mind, body, and spirit. The teeter-totter of past thoughts and present moments dizzied his thoughts. His hand instinctively darted towards the cockroach, bumped against the wall with a clasp motion, then cupped the little one into the soft skin grasp.

"No worries, little one," he whispered. "I know you just need a little air. Let me speed your journey." He stood up, hand cupped, walked towards the wall window.

"Knock, knock, knock," the apartment front door called at him again. He ignored it until after this immediate mission call achieved completion.

The window was already open, as he needed to keep it

so, for attraction of fresh air flow into his tattered and dust magnet abode. His fingernails, long and thick, he used to lift up the window screen.

"Aero flight or pedestrian brick wall travel today?" he inquired of his little antennae friend. He sensed aero, unfolded his hand and fingers, and the flight to find family began for little one. Given the direction of the scaley wing flutters, the destination was a hunter green garbage dumpster at the alley's end. The wind currents were favorable to such a trek.

He had to grab each hand towards each of his eye ridges to massage the skin, to awaken it into a pre-dawn morning light about to morph into full dawn. He rolled slowly his eyeballs in the sockets to flex and massage the surfaces and activate them to full operational ability. Took in a deep breath, first through nostrils and then through the mouth cavity, after sensing whether any atmospheric might attempt an invasion of alley detritus.

"That felt darned good. Now who is so patiently knocking at my front door?" He wondered, but his nasal inhales provided a petulant hint.

He walked over to the door, unlocked it, and turned the handle, sniffed an aroma he recognized as devoid of malignment danger, and pulled the door back towards himself. He didn't even look at the woman who entered. His keen nasal activity told him as soon as the first door rap engaged aromatic senses. As she stepped inward, he moved the door slightly towards her. She bumped her head against it and a soft fleshy compression sound vibrated into his right ear cavity.

"Dick," she word darted towards his ear.

"Sorry," he chuckled forth. "No Dicks here."

"Your insincerity is near equal to your arrogant ignorance," she audibly flung back. "And that shoulder slouch. Does it never end?"

He forced his shoulders back, straight, or at least straighter, then relaxed them into his normal slouched gait position. To forego his anatomical construction for the sack of humanoid visual clarity seemed uncouth.

"Ouch. Too many words too early," he moaned.

"Oh, your poor brain. What took so long?"

"Had to let my little roach mate outside."

"Or maybe an irresistible urge in that dream of yours," she scolded.

"What?"

"You talked in your sleep."

"No, I couldn't have. I wasn't talking in my dream."

"Irresistible urges are diseases," she stated authoritarian in nature.

"Says who?" He nervously wondered in barely audible tone.

"Me." She seemed certain in tone.

"Well, I guess that settles it, huh."

"Whatever."

"Who's this whatever? Should I be jealous."

"Do I get a seat today?" she voiced as her daily increment of sarcasm had yet to become exhausted..

No further words interceded into the dank room air currents.

Then, "Two wooden nickels for your thoughts," he playfully knifed the dead airtime.

"You need to stop living on country boy time," she hurled to him as insult.

"I'd rather live two lifetimes in the city, than the otherwise notion you posed," he spoke in a sincere tone.

"Have you ever considered your woeful inadequacy to perform necessary tasks?" She looked around the room which bore more a resemblance to the City dump landscape than a dwelling of immediate humanoid occupation.

"Sure. Often."

"And?"

"Nothing. Oh, how's my research going?"

"Touché. As your assistant, I must say progressing as usual."

"Great. Detailed and on time."

"Of course."

His senses told him she left out some crucial and curious facts.

"Something troubling you?" he asked. He noticed by her immediate facial and body demeanor change, a measured awareness of her discomfort.

"There are actually a few red flags."

"First," he requested.

This group hired by your benefactor has worked together previously, at least some of them."

"Second."

"Death always rears its ugly head when they are teamed up."

"Death. Got it. Anything else?" Always something else.

"The party in the group who always meets their maker is a journalist."

"Well, we are each journalists, and you aren't traveling with us, so you should be okay." He noticed she still seemed concerned.

"One last thing," she intoned.

"Go."

"Well, you know how thorough I am."

"Right. And the one last thing?"

"I researched you, just out of curiosity, since this employment journey reflects on my skills for future opportunities."

"I understand, and . . ."

"Well, I couldn't find your name in the City birth records."

Silence reared its ugly sound again. He thought about a response which would convince her of his legitimate purpose.

"I . . . am . . . a ghoul."

She laughed, not nervously. Then spouted, also not nervously, "That's a good one."

"Yes. Works all the time."

They mutually laughed. He dug the conversation trench downward a bit deeper, to bury the legitimacy of such a thought.

"Been around for about two hundred years. Important work it is. Important. Odd thing is, I don't remember much about my early life. Perhaps when this whole job thing we are working on ends, you can help me discover more about myself." He noticed her body tensed more than a bit, as if punched in the gut. Silence droned on again, until he cracked it like a hen's egg, the juices and orange-yellow yolk spilled out, awaited creation form orders. Omelet, scrambled, sunny side up, over easy floated amidst his mind cells, pinched hard by appetite unquenched.

"Hungry?"

"No, no, I'm fine."

He could sense she was not fine, at least in this moment. His words had boxed in her psyche too tight.

"Well, time for me to go."

Immediately his imagination spoke to him, "She's never coming back."

"Before you go, can you slide open that window a bit for me," he asked.

She stood up from the couch, walked over to the window, slid up the screen, and in flew his tiny cockroach friend, and a few companions, into her face gaze, fanned it lightly as the outdoor natural wind currents spun in tandem to the tiny insect wing twitters, but the little ones whizzed around the curvature of her right face cheek, and onto the wall above the couch.

She didn't screech. Instead, she froze in place.

His conscience reminded him not to be careless. Humans were an unconvinced biology bunch. Instinctively, they refuted observations about what their own senses told them, to allay fears, or at least bag them for ad nauseum rumination later. They scoured the environment for wisdom continuously, to the point of obsession. They lived amidst their own obsessions, almost cursed by such thoughts; chained by thoughts;

imprisoned by thoughts. A prison they richly deserved, these humanoids of all stripes, at least from a ghoul world perspective.

He moved, in a soft glide, towards the window and up against her back, in ghoul form, softer than human anatomy when such bodily adaptation required, as now, then laid his pillow soft and now translucent hands upon her body and coaxed it backwards into a flat prone position. She floated away from the window, no parts of her able to touch the floor surface, as he guided her onto the couch to lay. She remained tense, near immovable physically. He felt badly.

He glided back over to the window, broke off a piece of the brick exterior, crushed it in his hands, then blew the sand-like remnants across the alley way and into the glass window exterior. He guided the red brick pebbles to click along the window glass. A resident, elderly woman, came to the window. He asked in whispers if she could play the piano keyboard portion of "Layla" by Derek and The Dominos. The elderly lady, his friend since the time he had moved in several months ago, was deaf, but she could read his lips as well as she could read music, and play the music better, as she had studied piano and played in the local symphony orchestra, part-time, to make ends meet. She went over to the piano at her far interior wall, sat on the bench, slid up the key lever protector, and softly played.

He sucked in the sound as much as possible, then breathed it into the interior air of his apartment. The effect was so stimulating, the music notes themselves seemed to appear over his researchers head. She seemed to calm down a bit, in a daze. The mouse in the bottom of the couch, too, became aroused, and crawled out from under the couch and then up along the sofa arm edge, crossed the arm and brushed against her red head. She wasn't disturbed, yet. The impromptu piano serenade ended. The sudden silence awoke his woman friend from her haze. The mouse jumped in the air as if to clap. She had become revived enough to see the mouse falling towards her face, and she involuntarily screamed, mouth wide open.

He rescued the mouse friend from her gaping mouth cavity, his hand still translucent in appearance as it captured the mouse body only an inch from her gaped mouth darkness. A pleasant sight to him, but for her, a horror of horrors, at least judged by her reaction. She fainted. The daylight now in full flux, he realized he screwed this whole scene up pretty badly. She would leave and never return.

He tried to remind himself to not fear the Reaper. He had not been called yet. He still had time. The Reaper could trap him, for a while, and all of his existence purpose would become less relevant, abled for capture. He hoped to ask her advice to find an escape from such predicament. She slowly revived, then awoke, then spoke, in a weak tone.

"I'm sorry. Petite mal seizure. Not sure what caused it."

"Oh, no, no. Glad I was here to help."

"Gotta go. More work to be done."

"No, no. Your work is to rest now. And you, too."

She heeded his advice. Her strength had yet to fully return. He seated himself at the work desk, across to the room's dimmer side. Reflected a bit, to clear his mind.

Neighborhood birds began their own symphony in concert with the morning light. The bird tone helped him to materialize in a more solid and human form, more familiar to her gaze. He sensed something about her but unable to identify the meaning of this mild jolt, abandoned an immediate attempt at any further understanding. Work thoughts interceded.

Note, rewrite, delete, or incorporate. These steps served common deeds of authors, he thought to himself. Muscles around eye sockets drooped weak; sleep mind beckoned; random thoughts rallied into a charge; forge onward commenced in painful formed bleats. Another self-conversation commenced attention as order.

Remember: non-articulated conversation words, i.e., narrative, are from perspective of journalist's thoughts. I'm the journalist on this mission story. Story is written from journalist's perspective, and too, he is the ghoul. I am the ghoul. So too, is or are one or more of the others? I'll have to find out.

Next, plot issues. Journalist (I the ghoul) and also deeds Chronicler, finds the expedition members recommended by the Leader and interviews them, explains the mission, but not in detail and not exactly about what they are really looking for. Do they have dual credentials of scientific experience, i.e., is each experienced in more than one science category, in the event one of them dies or is injured or goes missing?

They've been assigned to different planes for this reason. He wondered. I wondered. So, if one plane crashes or some of them don't reach site destination, then those on another plane can take their place? What if one of them figures out the planning precautions, then exploits it, kills off one or two to increase their monetary compensation shares?

What if the team accidentally finds an unknown ancient civilization? And some of the civilization's descendants have survived, deep underground, or in a vast cave system? What if I notice characteristics of strangeness, at dig site? When the team finds the unknown civilization artifacts, there are footprints, not theirs, and someone in the group notices changes to the site after they have entered and returned to camp. Since I, the journalist researched the area history, I know about the mysteries of the area and what possibilities may be uncovered. Remember to obtain thorough research from my research assistant.

Rust and Ash

Strange thing about life. Sometimes good memories evolved into bad ones, and bad ones remained as the only good ones left, to stand erect among ash piles. "Just another assignment." He kept telling himself such. But it wasn't. Too much research for this one, even for his calling as a journalist. His employer, Hermann Sorenson, requested detailed and specific background information for each targeted participant. Participant in what endeavor, he wondered still.

His assistant, by all standard measures, ranked average in modern day appearance standards. Average height, average weight, neutral hair color of the red-haired genomes class, limbs average. Yet, something about her struck a musical chord in his chest, and once the string plucked, his mind begged control of the feeling, as intense feeling levels strayed his course.

She had entered upon a knock but not call of acknowledgement, or did she? Was his mind playing the tricks attributable to a half-awake mind of the moment previously referenced? It was just like her, enter at will. A danger, he thought, not just to her, as she didn't know in what state of mission preparation he had entered or just existed, and further, dangerous for him, as he had long ago realized he needed her, although for reasons of economy and efficiency, resisted all accreditation except thank you words spread mainly upon the fine plates of her favorite Italian restaurant.

They were a team effective, but to acknowledge such was not his business when research assistants disappeared or became disabled in ways indelicate.

He realized imbued she existed with chutzpah to test his mettle, which she relished to do by his notice, so he let her administer the tests. At first, he passed them easily, these feats of mind and physical accompaniment. But verily, she devised tests, exams, more difficult, challenging, and even intriguing to his mind. He began to wonder if she was mere human, a hybrid, or another under world or other world entity. He evaluated configuration skills, to his mind and experience, qualified for Teacher status, or even Trainor.

And for these reasons, and one other, his like of her persona, grew, bloomed, and flittered along the sharp edges of the cavern of failed romantic love. He avoided her for extended periods of time, in the hope he could forget prior events, relationships, lessons, as less knowledge, in the initial phase of such interactions bore sweeter fruit in appearance.

The fates that summoned him to love, like, admire her at first evolved into thoughts as flagrant and mistaken. After much similar experiences, he began to realize some substance to these moments and the accompanied events, enough so to avoid the eventualities during his work.

He directed his mind to describe what is exotic, tempting, elusive, intoxicating, powerful in her. Eyes that bored inside the brain of anyone captured by her glance, then stare. Her hair strands that worked like a spider's web, pocked of flitters, covered by revolutions of thread, remarkably hypnotizing in design, entranced him. At borders of head hair emerged birth-planted seeds of red tone.

A face, which he had previously designated ordinary, yet upon closer and near-term familiarity inspection, beamed as classic beauty, the lines near perfect at jaw line edges. Soft light skin, down to the pores surface. Her nose, strong yet lean, a sight hint of a knob near the joint at the spot between the eyes. Anyone brave enough to capture her glance knew a distraction magical. The looker's vision back and forth at each eye, hypnotic in effect.

He could not often reflect upon her lips and mouth overall as he feared moments of mind loss, uncontrollable fascination in the places where he imagined it soft warm. To avoid the tongue at all costs, his cardinal rule, as she appeared to have become skilled, as if through rigorous practice, at conjoining her tongue movements from attach point to narrow tip, especially when extended beyond her lips outer surface. The chin perfectly meshed into an exquisite oval of her facial structure, from frontal and side appearances symmetrical. A rare feat as if carved the gods of nature. He had spied such an anomaly biological among his own home clans, but not in the humanoid world.

"Why do I connect so with this humanoid?" his mind inquired, a bit in the nervous streak vein.

For these reasons, and for the mere contemplation of such thoughts, he seriously considered terminating her, as he feared she was a threat to his preparation skills during long research periods. He noticed visions of her face, body long in stature yet pleasantly lean, although he knew her to be strong in muscular appearance as he had picked her up a few times at the public gym where she worked out. Her hips were a bit wide but of no concern visually. He guessed she had been pregnant at least once, yet the topic never entered discussion, as it didn't need to.

They were co-working on varied projects of concern to their prospective employers in varied capacities, such as intricate background investigations of potential employee hires, physical plant security issues, and similar employer generated projects.

He assessed her mettle, at the gym, orally.

"Who's your buddy?"

"I'm my buddy," she simply responded.

She passed his test, and he doubted her functional abilities less after that moment..

Perfection deemed over-rated, by his own mind. Such goals resided in manager mind haunts. Rats lived there in thought scratches. Adopted, when noticeably young, before his memory was enabled to grasp varied nuances, he started a trek to identify his familial history, yet successful conclusions evaded the efforts.

His senses had always streamed heightened, more so than those of others around him, he noticed. He didn't understand why, and eventually allowed it to not concern him. In his employer, Sorenson, he found a potential mentor of similar instincts.

"Don't mind the bodies," he joked.

"I don't," she responded, meekly.

He sensed her looking around.

"Death is as death deals …" his voice hummed, echoed, then trailed off.

She still seemed concerned.

"Don't worry. The finer vagaries of a woman's body still elude me, for now." He toked out a chuckle. She had yet to become relaxed about the misery scenery resting peacefully around her.

A mouse in the wall scratched a tune. He noticed she had noticed. So, he felt compelled to explain.

"My friend. The little one begs entrance. I've yet to trust her."

"How do you know it is her?"

He sniffed the air. "Smell. Smell tells everything about anything." Just her outer essence served well to fill him up and slay a deeper appetite necessity.

"All senses bare unmasking." To his line of thought, desperate to inject a sentient retort, else loosen the communication high ground, she blurted these words.

He nodded in respect, "Yes. Yes, they do."

His mind chain rattled, so loudly, he feared she could audibly perceive it.

"The bodies are mannequins. An artistic project, in progress."

"Refreshing to know," she responded.

Then he added further discontent to her uncertainty.

"Don't touch them," he counseled.

"Why?"

"They may awaken."

As he had grown in age and physical stature, the Reaper's tune played upon his mind many times more than once. He developed a dance to the tune, escaped capture. Never certain how he managed in these situations. Slowly, his hips swayed, first right, then left, then right, lastly left. His mind sought entry into memory land. Still, he sensed her buttocks sought a relaxed seating space on the far couch planted just inside the front window. But another and more immediate matter entered his mind.

He sniffed the air.

"What is it?" She asked, adding a confused look.

He sniffed the air again, tried to identify the origin point.

He looked around her, and about her, from top to bottom, side to side.

"That smell, aroma, as it were," he remarked.

She glanced him an uncertain look.

"Are you wearing perfume?

She noticeably tried to not look uncomfortable.

"No. Not usually, not now."

He stood up from the uncomfortable wooden chair and moved a bit closer towards her, just two steps. Directed a question towards her.

"Perhaps your laundry detergent, then?"

She pulled the curved neck area of her shirt away from her skin, then lowered her head and sniffed. The jaw line at the chin's apex unhid a ribbon thin fat layer at the inward inclination of her neck.

"Just me."

Irritated, she grabbed her crotch. Pulled upwards on it a bit. Smiled.

"No pees in a while either." She thought he might laugh at her words, or at least issue forth an uncomfortable smirk, but he seemed in a bit of a deep and calculated contemplation moment.

"I'm sorry. Just a bit worried," as he reseated himself, then continued, "Don't want you to be noticed, out in public, by anyone who might try to insert themselves in our work business."

"Understood."

"Did you complete the background investigations on the individuals I requested?"

"I emailed them to you before I came over. Just wanted to make sure you received them."

"Good. I slept in."

"I noticed. Your phone took a message."

He remained a bit stiff and not fully awake as the chair back gnawed at him.

"Maybe some stretching will help your body, and mind, to unwind into this new day," she suggested. "By the way, does the neighborhood always exude such a dank odor?" She felt uncomfortable asking.

"That's a thing, here. Sewage Plant not far down the road."

He noted she still didn't seem quite comfortable in the moment. He appreciated her questions. Helped his mind become stimulated towards a humanoid-like normalcy. He was a bit out of practice in that regard. She obliged a further conversational travel path.

"You need anything? Looks like you had a long night. Feeling okay?"

"Sure. Sure. At least I'm standing, err, sitting upright," he joked.

He thought about sushi. Raw fish ribboned tight in circles. Wasabi.

Strains

Inspiration reflected window stains of desperation. As a young boy, he eventually realized there was something odd about himself. Informed so by others. Made fun of by his friends for his unusual facial expressions. The boy in him made unusual expressions because he suffered headaches, like migraines which caused red and then green spots as they temporarily and nearly blinded him.

In these moments of agony, a much older male ghoul hand reached out, then another, then the hands cradled him. The eyes set deep into the face of the cradler glowed yellow. Other similar faces entered his view range, then morphed as invisible fingers stretched and pulled against the features. The face growled. He growled back. Then mutual howls and yelps serenaded his memory. They continued in sound until their resonance became mutual. Uncommon sounds reverberated, just before dawn, as if roosters crowed in unison. Preparations. Preparations for what, uncertain.

He suffered a very horrible and painful migraine while visiting his grandmother's house. He howled in pain. His family left him there for caretaking, and in the morning, he awakened as if in a hangover, barely able to keep his balance. The old male ghoul, his grandfather massaged the boy's temples and helped him relax. Grandfather told him a story about a humanoid Slavic legend involving people turning into creatures temporarily, depending on the weather, like right after rainstorms or thunderstorms.

One day, he fell, more like slipped while running in flip flops after a back-alley rainstorm left puddled up water running down alley. His physical landing point was chin which met harshly into the concrete alley floor which guided the water flow towards the storm drain. Exuding blood amidst a single deep cut to his chin, he tried to wipe the blood spurts but inadvertently directed them onto his shirt area at the chest. He ran home to his mother who screamed at the site of his profusely bleeding chin. The blood followed a gravitational path both inward and outward, thus moving into his mouth which ejected frowns. His mother grabbed a cloth from the kitchen, rinsed it in water, then folded it and tried to dab his chin to stop the bleeding, but it wouldn't stop, so he cupped his hands to stop the blood from dripping on the floor.

When the boy was fourteen, he still had his original canine teeth, and they are very sharp. Dad took him to a dentist who seemed perplexed by the sharpness of the teeth. Dad related to the dentist that his son grinded his teeth, a nervous habit. Dental x-rays revealed the two teeth must be removed, then the second set of teeth must be pulled downward, or they would grow in the opposite direction and cause severe facial damage.

Such were the images provided to his ghoul brain by clan decree, as means to provide some type of humanoid background experience in the event his clan needed to provide a family member of appropriate age for a travel expedition to a planetary system for to assess potential food sources, or to explore protection measures potentially needed of the clan world in the event of a humanoid attack. How to act like humanoids. Survival training.

"We have three lives," he surmised silently. The life inside our body, and mind, and minds of others. It is an internal life. Occupied only by the one in possession of the body and mind. We have another life which exists in the external to our body and mind world. It is the life which interacts with the atmosphere and objects and other living things where our feet plant, or the available limbs rest. Finally, we have the life which exists in the minds of others. The others, including animals and other species from micro to macro in scope, capture a piece of us in their own perception and physical ability skills, interpret who we are from their stationary point, as we cannot occupy it mutually on a cell-to-cell basis. Yes, there is intercourse, which binds the internal and external, however briefly, yet that connection point, cavern still remained solely owned by the individual entities.

"So, now I'm the Seventh Ratica, the generation of greatest strength amongst any given gene pool of creatures or humanoids, a ghoul who has re-awakened seven times to accomplish deeds of those who summon me," he thought, but at times wished to espouse in a reveille to the humanoid realm, which of course would result in certain death. He had no choice in the matter. Survival first, last, and always. His summoner remained uncertain in identity, as such a task remained to become resolved. The summoner could choose to use anonymity as shield. Of course, these rules applied to non-demon entities only.

Demons possessed the existence mechanism to connect all three of these lives, simultaneously, if only briefly. A brief amount of time to one entity may seem an eternity to another, depending on the conjointment circumstances. Ghoul and humanoid interaction time lengths depended on the lifespan of the humanoid summoner. To date, I developed the following data.

Team Members, pending Sorenson's approval, and recruited per necessary skill sets.

Seven scientists: Five men, two women.

All ingrained of significant flaws in thinking, tied to cardinal sins greed, gluttony, and more baser instincts. Apparently, you really can't save a planet's surface. You can only tolerate it. Whether their actions demonstrate wisdom or foppery, the jesters will decide.

Humanoids, and all creatures for that matter, were each alike. They only came around because the target had something they needed. Food, shelter, social comfort. In the evening, beauty of the spider's web gleamed amidst the moonlight. Don't touch it. The spider need's the touch, but not for companionship, and only for consumption needs, of the spider. Any living thing that broaches the web's beauty invites itself as next on the edible feast menu of the web's host. Such, too, is the pattern of existence extension. Urges, needs coalesce, until the mingled numbers inevitably multiply, at varied intervals, and not always suitable to the environment. But the environment always serves a last revenge act which usually ends in the sounds of scream. Whether these sounds result in mutual pleasure, pain, or transgress upon a one-way street in either direction, the night doesn't care, nor trifle in the machinations of matters sprung. The night exists merely as observer, for as long as observation time lasts.

Wildly exposed are the frailties of humanoid perspective, especially in darkness, and too, competition events. Every day journey from beginning to end mimics sport and limited visions. Time to trip the light fantastic. That is, dance, as in "Let's go out tonight and trip the light fantastic." This expression was originated by John Milton in L'Allegro (1632): "Come and trip it as ye go, On the light fantastick toe."
Team Member Background Information
(my notes, rough draft sim, potable Team Members)
The Chronicler, Scientist One, Aurelio Rodriguez
(aka, Aurie, that's me, name ending in "i", sometimes in "e". it's complicated. oh sheet. gotta' poo, or pee, or both. again, this humanoid stuff is complicated for me. i'm a seventh Ratica, that is, the seventh generation of my ghoul Clan species and for this mission, also chronicler of the hi-jinks.)
A journalist chronicler first, now, but educated in the sciences of biology and botany, and some medical training comparable to a humanoid EMT. But he is more than a journalist. He is a ghoul. Has inhabited the human realm for a few hundred years. He previously marked each of the other Team characters, including The Leader, Sorenson, with tattoo-like marks or blood born scars, through accidents he arranged for each as they were growing up. The tattoo on each gives the ghoul journalist a bit of power to briefly manipulate the mental actions which react with their bodies to create physical reactions according to the journalist's will. When he is horny, he manipulates women in this way. When he is angry during male-to-male encounters, he manipulates the aggressor to either get them to back down, or to cause them to slip or miss a punch or errant throw an object at him, including the shooting of a gun.

Only marginally living on the edge of the science world, studied biology and botany, went to school on an ROTC scholarship, served in the Army, learned combat skills.

But had become a journalist, essentially because he had drifted lazy in the science, did not keep up with it, and had a knack for producing the written word, so he was the observer and chronicler of the trip. He learned more about each of the others, while at the same time learning more about himself during self-imposed and regular introspection.

All the potential participants below have heard rumors about crazy things "The Leader" had done in the past, such as he was giving a speech at a college, and a protestor ran up on the stage and tried to stab him, but the knife slipped from her hand as she thrust it towards his chest but banged it into the podium microphone stem and the knife sliced off some of the fingers on her left hand. The audience gasped, some ran from the room in a near riot, but the few who remained witnessed "The Leader" Sorenson reattach her fingers during a secret prayer. Some event witnesses said they heard a language they couldn't interpret; Sorenson spoke in a voice that didn't seem connected to his lips or jaws, but banged around the room as if echoes, and then the knife thrasher's fingers reattached as if the tendons, skin, and veins were magnetized and attracted back onto the finger stumps.

The Leader, Scientist Two, Hermann Sorenson

"The great good awaits."

A man older than the others, primary area of science astrophysics? (still need to look them up. Is Sorenson the summoner?) He craved fame and fortune which never came his way. This trip was likely his last hope. Yet it was exploratory only and not perceived as production of any ground-breaking discovery or newly formed theory.

The Student, Scientist Three, Beth Brazile

A young woman intern possessed of an ability to examine the finest minutia and detail until it puts the others to sleep, yet her mind worked at high speed and 24/7, even when dreaming. She seemed destined to die at a youthful age, burnt out, as she lived and learned, intellectually at 100 mph minimum speed. Her obvious means of counter-weighting this curse upon her, was to talk slowly and deliberately. Some of her ideas were stolen by her mentor, but she relented and didn't make a complaint as she suffered from drug addiction fostered by fibromyalgia, an illness where the patient shows no signs of illness yet still feels much pain, off and on, and of no specific cause or origin implementation.

And she did not want to abandon or become extricated from her chosen career path over it.

The Dreamer, Scientist Four, Aaron Abraham

"My love for her was like a drug to me. It filled my soul. She left me for someone else. My passion for her still remained. Unrequited love is a cruel poison."

Middle-aged male, scientist of archaeology, medical doctor, cursed by loves lost obsessions.

The User, Scientist Five, Dirk Denizen

Chemist. Money grubber, like The Leader. Will steal or cheat to succeed, but not for fame in Denizen's case. Worship's economic benefit gods. Primary goals: really desired endless amounts of wine, women, and song on a large yacht, whenever and wherever he pleased. Grew up in such a life but squandered his inheritance quickly, through shoddy investments prodded from him by a thief of an attorney appointed to him in his father's will.

The Shiny Stone, Scientist Six, Katarine Pugh

"Wine is the fine that makes me give a dime," she toned.

Metallurgy and physics major, worked for global in size minerals recovery operation company; and medical internship, but did not complete her internship. Possessed of rudimentary medical skills, just bored she became and moved on to make some fast money.

The Money Man, Scientist Seven, Benedict Lemieux

Known as Ben, independently wealthy, bought his way onto the excursion by funding it. Minored in archaeology. Well-known celebrity as a person who wants much attention and fame. Funded many ground-breaking business organizations, all of which eventually failed within 10 years, but he used the capital from selling each business before it failed, to start his next financial adventure. Technically he is a scientist in education only, as he does not possess much research experience. He is an observer like Aurie, except only to the degree of determining whether there is a profit in the effort. Schooled in anthropology and history. He hires people to research the project, so he knows a lot about the environment he is technically invading in order to exploit it for his personal gain. Long ago his motive was to save the world, until he determined it could not be saved, no matter the effort; so, he determined to save himself and enjoy the ride along the way. Ben has learned much in the way of self-defense, knows his way around weaponry and knows how to use it. He brought along some explosives, guns, and knives.

Onward And Sideways

Hope is the fool's game we never tire of, fortunately. Good leaders don't intentionally create an environment poisoned by unpredictable chaos, but bad leaders tend to utilize methods of control that trend towards a form of dominance over the masses. Humanoid history need only be consulted for ample evidence instances. Every single governmental system in existence today uses this same method of social control as means to survive in power and cement further a control status. Poor communication greases the wheels of destruction. Lack of solicited feedback, or solicited feedback ignored tends to sour the fruits of an energetic work force.

The chaos element stems from the unpredictable nature of a system developed by the leader's minions. The minions are battalions of control, from upper management levels and down to humanoid resources monitors. Any employee who notes issues or problems, if that employee works outside the control group of the leader, is demeaned or punished for pointing out the obvious. The co-workers of the more sentient employee are subtly made aware of such punishments in order to maintain control over the entire group.

A more nefarious system amongst the management mongrels and their minions is to ignore the sentient employee's perspective, solicit such perspective, analyze and file the feedback, then after sufficient passage of time proceed to claim the valuable ideas as management's own stroke of genius. This circumstance unfolds some significant amount of time later, after management has tested the employee's methods, and determines it produces viable and more profitable potential. One of those management minions is then assigned to take credit for the idea, implement the new methods of procedure, then accrues financial and social benefit. The employee who presented the initial idea may be moderately compensated, but the truth is that same employee is then designated a threat to management power and control, and the ill feelings therefrom roll downhill until the employee who benefited the whole company system is shunted to the point of moving on to either another department in the company, or onto another company altogether.

The final and most desperate level of chaos implementation as means of control is to continually change the operations system, then claim the changes were needed to stay up with competition, or base the change methods on fake polls or surveys and promote the idea as customer demands. The employees tasked with implementing these changes know well whether the changes are helping or pleasing customers. The ground level employees interact with customers every day, unlike the managers who hide in near ivory towers and gullibly consume the upper management gobbledygook as means of survival of their own careers. But they are banned from making statements against the egregious aspects of the changes; even when the rebel of the employee group successfully tugs hard the earlobe of a management ally, of which there exists no such thing except in character play instituted by management to win respect and trust of the employees. Every aspect of the large work entities' operations is time tested, and thus researchable for the most likely and usual results.

Results, regardless of the time frame construct, is failure. But long-time failure serves only to bury the efforts in the dust bins of history. These dust bins are fertile ground for so-called new and innovative ideas, which are neither new or innovative but just forgotten, so to revive them appears on the business scene as heroic and novel in effect to those uneducated about the actual history which is sometimes intentionally buried to avoid disgraces of failure and immodesty. Science theories, social construct political machinations, historical data, paper media to Big Tech electronic operations, marketing commercial efforts; all examples of the antiquated slash new modern marvel construct. Many humanoids affected either directly or indirectly from these group control methods existed completely unaware of the system extant and acting as a living creature.

Aurie existed as living creature, not completely humanoid except in appearance, and trained so from birth. Still, more creature than otherwise, as ghoul. The training forced him to exist well-aware of the humanoid constructs, much better trained than the humanoids themselves growing up in those environments. Command and control essence more valuable as greater knowledge and better implementation in actions based upon such humanoid born fruits. Tasty and enriching mind and body meals awaited.

Some additional caveats, to survive the employment conundrums. Speak to management when they have made themselves ready to listen, but at least one essential caveat applies here. The most sentient of employees knows to say what management wants to hear. Mental digestion of the books and electronic materials management uses, such as specific to the business entity management training manuals, and learn the essentials of management theory, which will lead to a more compatible work relationship. Delicately and respectfully mask complaints as suggestions noble. Sometimes they will feign a listening interest. Remember too, silence is golden allows for longer survival periods, in the office, and in the jungle.

Last caveat. Books and internet sources could serve merely as propaganda promoted by those who held onto a puppet master's strings of power. Us puppets needed to be smart about usage of such machinations. Learn how to navigate them as defense and advantage.

No different than aforementioned operational means or methods reviewed in management theory, Sorenson constructs of operations lived. Once the exploration Team arrived in Antarctica on a small island near the mainland, they started to explore. The terrain essentially acted as part of a frozen mountain which jutted high from the surrounding ocean currents. Much of the mountain scape lived below the ocean levelling point.

I became bitten by something, as diagnosed by Katarine, the wound swelled, like a large mosquito or spider bite, then mysteriously receded and I recovered. As Chronicler, afterward upon rest, I noted the circumstance of the situation from locale, bite moment, and recovery time. I began to realize perception skills increased in intensity for me. I heard, viewed, understood better, perceived better, almost able to accumulate pre-cognition episodes as if I could now discern likely future actions and their results upon the expedition group. Each time an instance of action commenced, it fit into my premonition mode, ticked off boxes, yet everyone I dutifully informed in the group corrected and scolded me at some point for being correct so much, to the point where a natural mocking effort commenced.

My consistent correctness failed to entrench an admiration and evolved into a liability. I learned to use such a reaction as shield, which allowed a quick probe of the actor's motives. I'd ask questions I knew the answers to in order to extract the perspective angle of the questioned subject. The downside engendered a continued mocking as less intelligent. A significant strength use, from my perspective. Pump the group's overconfidence. Such pumping clouded the Team's sentient perceptions about what could happen next.

Mission Creep

The expedition teams utilized two planes for the trip to the exploration site as precaution in the event only one of the planes completed the trip. Some members of the team on each plane noticed this issue, and wondered about safety of passage and any hazards perhaps they were not alerted to by Leader Sorenson.

One of the planes experienced a mechanical issue, veered off track due to magnetic waves in the area, and landed about 100 miles away from the plotted meeting point. When they disembarked, strange creatures were encountered. The pilot radioed this information to the other plane Sorenson and Aurie occupied. Aurie became aware of the situation as he heard the radio transmission. Aurie could hear the panic tone in the call. The creatures were described as mutated versions of the known wildlife in the area. Speculation about radioactive contamination ensued.

Sorenson's plane managed to land closer to the proper destination coordinates but also experienced unusual weather conditions related to odd wind currents and heavier than expected snowfall at ground level. A hike to the preliminary campsite remained.

Team banter became marked by dark tones.

"Actual actuality actually irritates irritatingly irritation."

"No, I know, my nose itches in bitches."

"Rich."

"Moments in time cannot be erased."

Only the memory of them may disappear, Aurie thought. Their voices studied the scene of no particular pattern certain.

"The problem with getting older is the length and breadth of knowledge encased in the brain cavity. It becomes so vast; the processing of the data takes a bit longer to categorize. A sound, a smell, a vision require placement into storage places, either as known or unknown. It is the unknown which spins and grinds the wheels faster and harder until a solution is found."

"Solution?"

"Yes."

"For what?"

"There are places in our mind where we seek refuge, warmth."

"What is refuge and warmth?"

"That is a question only you can answer for yourself."

"Whatever you make of it; whatever makes you feel safe, cozy, escaped from the complexities and anxieties of life's sound and fury."

Their own march of footsteps towards the campsite mimicked noun and verb displacements into the cool air. Once at the sight, Aurie set up a campfire in progress, as the others unpacked and arranged for impending daylight activities. Night noises announced a prescience of their presence. The humanoids could not help but begin words projections as shield against the night's unknowns.

"The sound of a night stream reflecting moonlight."

"Only ask why if you want to explode that comfort thought."

"Or perhaps, a why ask, is a comfort thought."

"Yes, perhaps it keeps the wheels comfortably churning."

"To a migraine mind, almost any sound plunks like a hammer tong."

"The spit of flame shards from this camp fire may ring sweet to the eyes and ears, or split untamed as shouts and screams."

"Creatures of this night are hunting. Others, the prey, are dying."

"Life goes on."

"The eternal wind, yes."

"Disfunction churns neither as travesty or trepidation."

"It just is."

"A justice random."

"A result certain, really."

"Even uncertainty is certain."

"Their resides rest in the chaos, even among lions."

"And snakes."

"And demons."

A howling echoes among the tree trunks in the distance.

"Apparently, someone among us isn't who they seem."

"Or what they seem."

No particular level of concern swayed among the group. Another problem to become solved had reared an ugly head, and they would stamp it down, tamp it away, as every movement of required doom dismayed.

"This place looks like another dimension."

"So, you've been to one?"

Aurie chuckled.

"Ah, our author researcher has some enlightenment for us."

Aurie thought, then spoke.

"Yes."

The team's hard laugh lightened the mood load a bit. Aurie's mind drifted away from the banal banter.

Dark Matters

Life existed in the nuances of moments. Many are ignored, like the edge of a cliff. Safe footing existed just centimeters away from certain death falls. Stability rested upon a grain of sand. She was just too good to be true, and that's exactly how it turned out. The most reliable curse you can expect of a humanoid is they will lie to you.

A dank smell pinched up his nostrils amidst quiet wind calm. The lack of wind failed to betray an origin stench source. Early morning sounds entered from the bedroom window. He rolled over towards her to find the bed empty, except for where his body and limbs rested. She was gone.

He focused on a sound nearby, farther away than the chirping morn birds. A swish and more swishes. A light line, straight, then peeling back emanated from the far wall. The bathroom door was slightly open. He sat up on the edge of the bed, stared at the floor to separate the carpet from the clothing dropped in the previous night and pre-dawn morning hours. A path to walk existed, to avoid detritus of rolled and splayed under garments. In the crooked display of cloth, he noticed his under pants, unrolled them, put them on; made it over to the doorway; pushed slowly open the door. Steam blankets floated under the ceiling. The shower window also betrayed a steam cover. He heard a high-pitched hum. Hypnotic it droned in tone and rhythm. A light air caressed his neck from behind.

Darker Matters

"You haven't lived until you've opened a box of cornflakes and noticed near about a third of the way down into it, seated on top of the lonelier flakes, is perched a roach, glad to have shared in the breakfast bounty."

"What would you do next?"

"Depends."

"Depends? On what?"

"On whether I move the friend out of the way, or spill it into the sink, watch it scamper, as I turn on the garbage disposal switch."

"Oh no you didn't."

"No. I didn't."

"What is that noise?"

"The neighbor."

She moved over to the side window, looked out through the glass, then gazed down towards the sound origin. He noticed her pants tighten along the curve of her buttocks. Tingles tickled the inner recesses of his brain, in places not quite yet familiar to this place where his feet were currently planted firm.

"Oh."

"Sounds like he's dragging another garbage bag. I could speculate aloud about the bag's contents, but it may alarm you."

"Your speculation or the bag's contents?"

He didn't respond, which acted as response enough.

"Scary," she mused aloud.

She came back to her couch seat which still displayed the round indenture of a taught buttocks print. As she bent her lower frame to perfectly plant back into the buttocks print, his voice offered counsel.

"Scary? That's not scary. Scary is watching a spider creep on spindly legs across an object, twig, wall corner, bed cover, then you glance away just for a moment, then retrace your gaze back towards the spider point, and notice it is no longer there."

"Where is it, then?" She asked.

"Anywhere, everywhere, in the tiny crevice, a space perhaps least suspected."

We all have a vibe that, once tapped, brings life to our insides. Eruption corruption, perhaps, it is.

"When an old Slavic woman tells you don't get on the plane, don't get on the plane!"

To follow one is to follow all.

To follow oneself is to lead by design.

Campfire Commiserations

Those who still remained played a game to lighten the burden of anxiety.

"Well, you've got two choices. Get out, or you can die."

One asks, "If you had to choose among two emotions, fear or sadness, which would it be?"

The Ghoul journalist, responds, "Fear."

They laugh and pipe up, each with a negative jibe.

He responds, "I've known deep sadness. Deep."

He explained how he had to put down his cats at the vet's office, laid each upon the surgeon table, due to no more money to take care of them. Alive furs and furls, Liz and Meg, injections of the death serum that put them to sleep still stung in his mind. He was allowed to pet them until their last breath. He thanked the Vet for kind assistance.

Sadness hung heavy upon his brow, wrinkled, and shriveled as wetness pockets breached over vision bows, then streaked random into threads.

He tried a hold back of tears as he left the room, walked across the main foyer, and out the front glass doors. Each step towards his car, the sound of each shoe sole scrape upon the blacktop driveway, shredded away pieces of his heart like the grating of a rectangular block of cheese. He arrived at his car, which no longer seemed important to him. It should have still felt that way because it had helped him travel through and upon the sharp stones of troubled times. The anxiety in his heart pulled upon him until his gut felt like it had been ripped from inside of him, torn from his intestines. He opened the driver's side door, squatted, and plopped into the driver's seat, placed his forearms and hands upon the top portion of the steering wheel to allow for them to act as pillow to his strained forehead.

He couldn't hold back the breaking of the emotional dam. These moments haunted him for exceedingly long time periods, eventually eroding away much capacity to feel the pangs and longings of emotions of any sort. Shredded he had become from the realities of life, always forcing himself to cling onto the sentience rope upon which he would remain firmly grasped upon, at the hands, arms, legs, and feet. Not enough cash resulted in two lives lost.

He could not escape the long fall from the moments at the Vet's office. His mind swung back and forth between the realm of reality and the realm of escape fantasy. The campfire died, and too the stories. Random words from random minds.

A Plotting Of Events

An apparent polar bear type creature, or some kind of hybrid bear, became attracted to their camp one night, sniffed around Beth's tent area, but she was on her period, so the bear left, only to then scout about Auri's tent, and took him away. Some Team members alerted to the sounds arrived at Aurie's tent and found blood evidence splotched about the premises interior, but not on the ground. It was a very snowy night and there were drifts, some exceedingly high, so such difficulties complicated a tracking of any creature.

But a closer inspection of the tracks in the snow, performed by some alerted Team members, revealed the nighttime creature wasn't a bear, because the footprint patterns indicated the creature walked on two legs, not four. The confusion arose because the tracks were so close together. It appeared the tracks were made by two creatures.

The Crazy In This One Is Strong

"Describe the tracks," his mind counseled. "One of the party group likely has some expertise in the matter. Size, deepness, estimate of size of creature. What type of creature. Human-like, or gorilla-like. Use biological names. Need to look up.'

"But the tracks disappear from the landscape," his mind bumped him again, "before a point of entry from the forested area is discovered."

Is the two-footed creature not of this earth?

"Eventually, Aurie is the only survivor," his mind counseled, unconvincing in tone. Funny. I'm not a survivor, except biology-wise. Ghouls can die, but can also resurrect for an uncertain number of times as long as even a semblance of biological remains are preserved for a resurrection purpose. That purpose is usefulness, as determined by Clan elders. A genealogical necessity in the world where we originated. Some resources scarce as kindness. Anyway, onward, upward, and downward in this tale beckons attention. "Escape this thought pattern and get back to the matter at hand."

Not just yet. His mind interruptions seemed like a torture. "When The Fungi Sing", he remembered as a tune from his youth.

"Oh. I used to love this concert as a kid. The fungi are singing. Their sounds are rhythmic. Difficult to tell what they are saying to each other in extreme cold. Not dolphin screeches. No sperm whale echoes long and melodious. More like toots and poofs of same tone and syllabic generation. I could stay here all night. Don't want to disturb them or the music ceases into dreary silence like white noise echoes. Their poetic sounds remind me of home. Chance chants. Never rants. Melodies marvelous."

Calm of mind, he could now progress into the next work phase. Anyway, mind warp over. I'll file away the bear snatching incident in the event I need it to throw off the trail of Sorenson's dubious of mind Team members.

During exploration preparation, the exploration group became schooled by Aurie of a highly efficient system for exploring, obtaining data, sharing the info among team members and the central computer system for immediate analysis. Such measures would reduce the time of the project goals completion, which remained to find something, anything that could better be used to improve the human condition, such as reduce the paralyzing effects of diseases, or eliminate them altogether. Of course, the non-sentient viruses of the planet would resist.

The Team's food packs offered liquid food, which when opened triggered aromas and stimulated the imagination to allow senses an opportunity to translate what the eater desired in the type of food choice. Lemieux created and marketed the food packet, which accounted for his significant wealth. Any kind of food texture, smell, aroma, appearance imagined could be created in the human mind by using the packet of liquid chemicals. Life expectancies increased due to this nutrition injection system as the body used less energy to absorb and digest the food. The teeth are not needed to chew it; the stomach lasted longer because it didn't need to utilize much energy for digestion. Workers and those at leisure could become more efficient and productive in each endeavor.

List of supplies included high protein packaged food and body sterilizers/cleaners that are rubbed on body (takes place of body washings). They all needed working headsets of audio microphones to communicate at all times amongst each other in order to share data, coordinate research and deductions, and record all observations in a computer base for immediate analysis and oral briefing.

All supplies slated to be air dropped in advance by his research assistant. Items included consisted of mobile phones, portable generators, sources to power them like batteries, gasoline, and kerosene for varied energy needs such as light in the dark, food preparation, warmth in the cold atmosphere.

Also, predicting weather dangers. Almost forgot that one. Any aspect of preparation could strike as doom during the excursion. So far, during time of the expedition, not much snow expected. He double checked temps in that area of the world. He prepped for Antarctica, Canada, Alaska, or Siberia like places, as a precaution. In this world, the human and humanoid personalities flashed as unpredictable as the weather. Caution signs scattered about his mind.

Trek Log

"What was that we just encountered?"

"Smelled like a male."

"I thought female."

"Why does that matter?

The reporter, Aurie, says he has to relieve himself, a wet one. He walks off, as the others wait. Sounds in the woods around and about them erupt. He can hear the Team conversing about the noises.

"A scream?"

"A howl, like a fox."

"A growl, like a wolf."

One of them goes off, "I'll check," and he moves out in Aurie's direction, disappears into the forest.

A few minutes later, Aurie comes back. "All right, done."

"Wait, where's Benedict?"

"What?" Aurie asks.

"You didn't see him? He went looking for you. We heard sounds."

"Got worried," another says.

"It's the forest. I heard nothing unusual," Aurie says, and adds, "Settle down. We have to find Benedict."

"You didn't see him? He went looking for you."

"Or your dick," another says.

Laughter, some uncomfortable.

"Odd that someone is missing already, this soon into the excursion."

"Benedict can be a bit of a prankster."

"Maybe the pranks on him, and it's pay-up time."

"A little bit longer than never is a good bit of time."

"Or a little bit further than almost there."

"Keep up this banter, and we'll be discussing our favorite beer."

"Or arguing about it."

"Arm-wrestling on it."

"What, no wine tasting?"

"What's your favorite steak type?"

"Steak isn't a type."

"Sure, it is, like pork portions. High on the hog, or rind."

Too many trudges longer had tired the spirits, and discussion thereof.

"Benedict still missing."

"Something doesn't smell right."

"I got you there."

"No. I mean the air aroma."

"Like a horse just keeled over and died, then expelled bowel detritus from the hind quarters."

"Not good."

"Something's dead."

"It's a game of hopscotch."

"Watch out for the line shapes."

"A game without the hops."

"Or the scotch."

"Damn. We back on the drinking binge talk again?"

"Anyone notice the lady hasn't offered any sound to this word buzzing crapola?"

"She has a point."

"And a way with words."

"You mean away."

"No words mean a lot. Really."

"Approaching Sanity point."

"In three, two, one."

"Where'd that funky smell go?"

"The way of the world. Listen."

"Sounds like a library out there."

"And near as silent."

The lady makes a verbal offer to this horrid male word salad.

"Time to check out those books, gentlemen, or leave."

"She has a point."

Then the lady zeros in.

"That horse rind smell, and that forest devoid of sound, can only mean one thing."

The males are still silent. Perhaps they know the answer, the conclusion.

"We have found Death's Door."

"Death's door?" one of the men asks.

"Yes, the name of this place."

The men do the grunting expected to shoo away the essence of death.

"Okay, we need a volunteer to knock, or ring the bell, or give a shout, if we are to enter."

A bit of uncomfortable joviality sounds slowly and unnervingly pricked the atmosphere around them.

Ghoul Zone

Benedict remained MIA. But the morbidity of the scene does not displace itself from their mutual emotion shakes. The evening floats onward like waves upon an ocean beachhead. Still, the Team is sitting around a campfire, perceived as the only lifeline in this desolate place unfit for humanoids, except one, the journalist Aurie who now rests in his tent. Sorenson excuses himself to go back to his own tent, says he forgot something. Then one of the group begins to explain what he suspects.

They are searching or trying to coax out a creature or demon, not yet catalogued in Earth history. Myths and legends about this creature have only been recently discovered by Sorenson on earlier search expeditions. The creature doesn't yet have a biological name designation, except genus unknown.

"What makes this creature so special?"

"It harbors in its biology or chemistry a source of untold power, to hypnotize, immobilize, entrap a victim through aroma and sound echo location, which is why it cannot or has not been successfully trapped. It may even have the power to disappear or execute a camouflage system to make it near invisible except remnants of physical contact, as feet to ground, hands to objects imprints."

"You mean, it could be here right now, and we wouldn't know it?"

They began to look around at each other and behind each other, and up towards the night sky.

Suddenly, Sorenson appeared, as if from the center ground campfire.

"Just an illusion friends. I was back there but crept up in silence to a point all of you ignored in your vision perspective."

"You mean humanoids have this adept quality feature, yet we didn't know?"

"Absolutely. Some of the greatest trackers in history have learned such skills, and more. They just aren't taught to the general public."

Another of them spoke up. "Only military special ops know and teach these skills."

An ill wind knows only motion.

Sorenson then spoke up again. "And the creatures who know them and pass them down to their kin in each generation."

"And so, this exploration is a mission to find this creature, which is more likely to find us without us knowing it."

"What does this creature consider a food source?" The woman asks.

"Virtually any living creature, and if there are none available, any plant or animal creature."

"They don't eat often," Sorenson stated, "because their digestion system is very efficient."

"So, if there are many meals available, then most of us are safe," one of the men interjected.

The female advised, "Given the atmosphere and temperature, storage of kills is possible for lengthy time periods."

One of the males speaks. "We are essentially occupying the creature's refrigerator at this very moment, at least, in a distance a bit farther away from this fire."

"One caution I might add," Sorenson advised. "Given we don't actually know the creature's biology and chemistry, it seems highly probable one or more of us could be kin to this creature, unknowingly."

A few of them scream out in protest, "What? How so?"

Sorenson stared deeply into the campfire blaze. A crackle and spit from the center shot orange shards skyward.

"Each of you has been joined to this Team based on my research, which emphasized any genetic connection you and your family ancestors may have displayed comparable to the creature history I have developed during my previous expeditions."

One of the men spouted out, "You mean one or more of us are guinea pigs needed to attract the creature to us."

"I know some of your previous Team members died on these excursions over the last several years."

An eerie silence began to stab into the air, interrupted only by the methodical campfire spits skyward.

Everyone directed a gaze at Sorenson. He responded.

"Didn't anyone read their contracts?"

The woman raised her hand. Everyone bored a gaze directly at her face, and awaited explanation.

"The contracts guaranteed money, life insurance, medical insurance, disability insurance, simple and standard Expedition Insurance, but there existed one exception."

When she paused, the silence spoke for them loudly.

"If the creature is found, and it happens to be one or more of them, the family relatives agree to receive double the guaranteed money, but only if all the named family beneficiaries agree to allow the discovered creature to remain as property of Sorenson for use in continued experiments. In other words, one of the family members can bind the creature to slavery under Sorenson's dominion."

They, each in the group, began to seriously consider, silently, the ramifications of such family decisions. Visions of family members, their history together, wonders about whether a communal agreement could be carried out to permit a release of the creature back into the wild, or into society. In other words, they contiguously began to understand their survival, or lack thereof, guaranteed Sorenson's control over every aspect of the contract, including disputes and resolutions thereof.

"Well, there are less of us here now."

"We don't know that. Some could have survived the crash. We would know if the storm, then the avalanche hadn't blocked our path."

"Don't you remember?" Sorenson asked. "We heard the explosion, saw the smoke lift high into the air."

Another added, "Sure, no one could survive that."

One of them toned out, "Just what are we looking for again?"

The speculation ripened.

"A Wendigo, I bet," one of the males offered.

Group discussion of the merits ensued.

"Changeling," posed another male. "We need more firewood," and off he went into the darkness to seek out kindling and wood.

Aurie recalled, from his tented confines, hearing someone of them, of a woman's voice tone, or perhaps disguised as such a sound, had discovered a detonator and switch which could have been used to explode the other plane. The voice stated the journalist was informed, but Aurie knew such a conversation never took place with him. He wondered who had been with Sorenson. Aurie's senses seemed unable to detect an answer.

Back to the present, Aurie warned himself. The fire circle conversation continued.

"Maybe this creature is a god," one of the males posed.

Sorenson laughed. "It's quite possible God is a virus that eventually mutated into a Universe, thus making us humans nothing more than gradually evolved and advanced viruses that mutated into a more sentient state."

"We are nothing more than chemical mush," the woman scientist teased.

"You mean we could all be residing in the liquid ooze of another species, extraterrestrial in origin, Petri dish, as it were. Mere cells experimentally, perhaps purposefully created, developed, then spread to the interstellar space winds."

"We use intellectual crutches to get through it all. Develop communities for protection; acquire, share and store knowledge; gather and harvest food development resources, as learned basic survival necessities."

"Protect ourselves, and others, to the potential point of complete annihilation," Sorenson warned.

"Every creature culture, species, does the same. There are no winners or losers. Only survivors."

"We are the hunters, and the hunted. The givers of life, and takers, too."

"A point helps to create a line, a line a curve, and a curve a circle."

"And every circle becomes a dimension swirl that forms a cone to lead back to origin point."

"I do believe we have flushed our minds of all necessary and immediate exhaustions," Sorenson jested.

"Wow. That montage was better than the best Carson," one of the men spewed out in a somewhat jovial manner.

"Carson?" the woman scientist asked.

"The late-night American comedian, on the old telly," one of the males quipped into the dark audio void.

"He's dead now, long ago."

"Some might mark him as philosopher."

"Split the nuances of humor, like Einstein split atoms."

"Similar results, too, intellectually," one of the males iterated drolly.

"Einstein didn't split atoms, but he learned of the procedure from his German counterparts," Sorenson noted.

"Technicality," one of the males said.

"Which runs us backwards into this moment, and our purpose here, to definitively uncover the mystery of this place and it's as yet undiscovered inhabitant, or inhabitants."

All heads and eyes within them swiftly turned towards Sorenson's after he uttered these words.

"Even our most jovial moments suffer mission creep."

"As they must," Sorenson said, and stated once more for emphasis, "As they must."

The rest of the group remains around the campfire, but something happens, or is described to happen, according to one of the fire spectators of the group.

"Look over there, but not directly, just from the corner of your eyes."

A few of them glance.

"Oh," she says.

(I don't immediately recall her name, only her scent, Aurie thought, as he spied the group from afar.)

"What?" asked the skeptical male.

"Yes. I see it," says another.

"You mean them," another adds.

"Inter-dimensional creatures," Aurie scoffs silently to himself.

"Remember that spot. We can check in the morning for any evidence of physical presence," another states.

"Time for an accounting," another ribs.

"Or a song," another chides.

"Right. Poisonous plants, mythical creatures and beings, death," another jibes.

"Perhaps we, all of us, bear a connection to all of those you've mentioned," another says.

"What a skiffy bunch we are," Aurie poked silently.

"New species are uncovered every day on this earth rock," another says.

"This one tried to end itself early, as means to sooner start a new beginning."

Aurie could hear the protestations of plant life in response to sadistic humanoid movements. He wondered why humanoids would want to experience a crazy assed plant afflicted by mouth-shout syndrome baritone onward. Not hearing meant not knowing, he surmised. Reminders of love-like feelings for his research assistant strangely broke the chaos curtain. He enjoyed being with or near her; became somewhat sorrowful to see her leave, walk away, when their moments together ended. Filed this moment away for future reference research. A thought shout rang out, rattled in his brain pouch.

"Maybe she is protecting me, as well as assisting in research?"

Damn how love bites. I remember you, from far away, in the mirror, in the day. Tripping over thoughts. Unable to escape. Get away, get away. Other matters in which to partake. Only death gets in the way of further thoughts of you this day.

He mentally composed some poetry in order to escape thought loops of her face, her aroma, her body movements.

Types of shit (shat, skat). Little log, big log; swirl, droplets, pancakes; each shows states of biological status, of the creature or humanoid. Shape, smell, location of placement, each shows a physical and mental status. Safe, fear, hurry, worry.

Okay. Stop, mind. Analyze the now. The creature they are tracking doesn't display skat results upon the ground. Perhaps it is buried to keep away predators or the curious. Some creatures forced to eat skat, or their own skat, to survive, or they take and move other creatures' skat to confuse trackers.

When nature does its thing, it destroys all thought incompatible biologically with continued existence priorities. The grand design rules, as edible protein searches become primary targets, while threats to continued existence lurk close by in the mind cavity or instinct pouch. Much like the human or humanoid existence history. The idyllic is a myth promoted by idealists who tend to create and recreate reality as needed to hold onto their view of power and control. Every clash of mind thoughts didn't necessarily require immediate resolution.

An "I and We" moment interceded. Protested at his attempts at present task evolution.

"Well, you're lying, cheating, stealing, crooked son deserved Hell. If you don't like that I removed a flea from this 7.8 billion hairs of the flea trap, I'd be happy to oblige your trip straight to the designed destination on the fast train."

"Do you realize who you are talking to?"

"Sure. Sure, I do. Just another Flea Lord on this bloody stream of suck ups."

"Well now. You've blown your cover. For whom are you working?"

"You wouldn't believe me if I told you. Besides, you already know. Just another question to enlighten the unenlightened."

A group member's voice pulled him back into the current reality.

Another of the group says, "Seems to me we're just food for the primary predator."

"Who is?"

"The boss."

"The Janitor."

Some laughter escapes into the moment.

"And the Janitor is?'

They take a second look at each other, then a few of them inadvertently but in perfect timing stated emphatically.

"The journalist."

Silence reigned once more, interrupted by intermittent foot stomps and slips amidst the living vegetation.

"Where, where is the journalist?"

A Dett moment rudely interrupted Aurie as the Team conversation receded in his mind to a background tone.

What in the furking furk does "In The Bottoms" mean?

See Dett's "In The Bottoms/Prelude/Night". Searched the mind catalogue, he did. What Bottoms?

"See Definition, 1. The deepest or lowest part: the bottom of a well; the bottom of the page. 2. The part closest to a reference point: was positioned at the bottom of the key for a rebound."

Sure. That cleared it up, but not the grabby vegetation aggravation even in the least. His mind continued an earlier moment self-flagellation.

"Why would you provide to me the presence of a woman I desire to ravish, yet poison me with the knowledge she would show no appreciation for it. Another curse."

"No. No. Not ravish. Just experience."

Must be a ghoul in this group, besides me. Reeks of one devilish in plans and palpitations devised by a group of Clans. Maybe more than one. Next thoughts, please.

Political parties imported illegal and criminal and militarily armed drug cartels into the major cities, who then became "off the record" enforcers of humanoid slavery trafficking and debilitating drug product infusions into the populace, thus creating a compliant and undefended swath of humanity subject solely to the political leaders' dominion. Profits from illicit ventures and murderous activities laundered through politicians' coffers, then distributed outward as "help" to a drained of energy populace. Anyone or group who complained or resisted this societal construct tempted social obliteration at the dirty hands of select government agencies designed to protect elite pedestal structures.

Destroy slavery resisters from the ground up. Deserved punishment for their insolent bondage resistance thoughts. Favoritism ruled the day, in any means or manner imaginable. Sale of mind, body, and soul resulted from first moment of birth to last breath of death. Assured a proper measure of food and shelter in order to survive, but the proper part depended on influence potential. Influence fueled humanoid desires. An easy pot to slow simmer and stir.

An orchestral concert of Big Media and Big Tech organized entities, assuaged populace tastes easily and readily, controlled under threat of societal cancellation, or permanent isolation from societal structures. Government overlords controlled the heat settings. Citizens real and imagined learned or were brainwashed to fear starvation of such cultural machinations beginning at a noticeably young age by their teachers. The kids simply had not chance to resist. Learn who to hate, including themselves and all of the prior generations of their families, and in return to place the government in the role of family. Government is master and good. Obedience to is the cardinal rule.

Universal examples abounded and bounded like microscopic atoms. Yes, in other worlds, macroscopic atoms existed, too. Uninhabitable they existed, by humanoid existence standards. Still, observable, but for what purpose such worlds existed remained mystery. Government showed films, basically produced and directed by movie makers, hired by the benevolent government to show crimes committed by masked citizens, and sometimes the facial features were changed of the criminals to make them look like people the government didn't want around any longer. Then those people became deemed to have recanted their crimes and sins and voluntarily agreed to mass suicide as punishment, in order to court restitution resolution in the next life. Such movies always showed a final scene of the guilty transgressors against good government to appear as voluntarily jumping into a large acidic container built to look like a river or lake where they atoned for their sins. End editorial mind dump. Flush.

Intercession Progression

I've come to check the noise. The noise about something. A mystery it remained, as no cause for it rendered a display of factual data. This noise in the house could have echoed from a lower room, or back room. I decided to exit my bed, after slight escape methods calculated from the blanket covers briefly intervened, searched around for the sound origin point while descending the staircase, but the noise eluded my mind in this immediate circumstance of moments. Perhaps a little gray creature, poking around for crumbs. No sound of tiny claws offered a conclusion.

Possibilities existed given past such events experienced by me. A cold dampness straightened the hairs on my skin. An aroma of dankness pervaded the lower landing. Having caught the naughty only minutes earlier, my left hand seemed attracted to the dampness as a twin aura. A reach forward of the hand attracted like a magnet the origin point of my concerns. The kitchen beckoned as destination. The young pin oak branch fingers, young in pin oak time yet tall still, stroked against the upstairs bedroom window, encouraged by a light night wind breeze, refreshing in the daylight, haunting amidst even partial moonlight.

Perhaps every seeker of knowledge earned what they deserved. Satisfaction or disappointment, whenever the front door opened and nothing found, the nothing entered as invited in bounds. For every pleasure so too existed a pain or more to gain it, grasp it, wring it dry like the over-wetted soggy sponge. Wedding bells gonged in refrain. Moment and taste intertwined as a holy vine of berries edible, grapes wedded and readied to be bedded. Inner loins panged against inner cloth linings. Silent biological sounds and motions guilty at the ready.

Then clear skies preceded by torrents of rain. The clouds, the in between, the vision I longed to see. Every median showed a flank of inapposite rings, bush thorns, and lily fields of range.

Hell hounds, dogs of war. What are you looking for? A meal, or something less real. A thought, or sentience, or naught these things of hope or strain. Perhaps a chance to sow the grain into fields barren, later to become shorn for the natures of life, and the quaint of the born. Ends always come, any time or place, too short or too late, as the same look of contentment glares in the dark space, the crypt or the grave or the urn gaily planked. From ghosts of ghosts we meekly descend, for a time, then to unknown descents. Second chances not guaranteed, nor the brazen courage displayed by the countryside weed. King, peasant, corporate CEO, clerk. An eternal dog's bay served as horn to the wary, sacred as moments of mirth and merry songs.

Not Again, aka, Just One More Time, Never

When you get to a certain age you appreciate more a satisfying meal, but afterwards some corollary issues arise like an ugly head premonition during sexual practices. Whether and how an internal organism will respond within you stabs. Always a mystery, it seems. A mystery pervasively resolved, but resolution mode means everything.

Okay. It becomes a three-ring anatomy circus. And the clowns create laughs to mask the misery of it all. There's a stabbing moment of seeing it all, each ring of the circus all at once, yet seeing nothing at all, as the mix portrays distractions, extractions, permutations of visual doubts. Remember what you want to forget. Curse. Forget what you want to remember. Curse.

"Did I just see that?"

"How'd that happen."

"No way."

"Way."

"Fright."

"Spite."

"No. That's too tight."

"Yuck."

"Sucked."

"One person's puke humor is another's sheer delight."

"Oh, the cuts. Oh, the streams. Bled by lonely dreams. Bred by homely schemes."

"We are all alone, even in large crowds."

"Walking all in shrouds."

"Alive dead. Dead alive. The borders of each world worthy of neither lows or highs."

"Halos abound among pincers of sounds."

"What's up and what's down shrinks in resounding circles. Lifts like translucent bubbles where our minds become captured, then ejected upon an accompanied pop sound."

"Pretty much every living thing is a tyrant, demanding control of their own environment. The problem arises when those oppressive individuals perpetrating such activity evolve into an extension towards those around them, within their sphere of influence. That's where the energy cord needs severance from the source, as the source has become a curse of inhuman capacity."

"Is that Bible wisdom?"

"Well, the Bible is ancient science fiction."

"Science fiction didn't exist at that time."

"Sure, it did. Called religion."

"Beings from another world, off planet, communicated with humans and humanoids, for the purpose of enlightenment."

"For the purpose of control."

"Control is enlightenment."

"Sure, it is. Just ask Mao, Lenin, Stalin, and pick your Roosevelt."

"Should we explore the Romans, Greeks, Chinese Dynasties, British Kingships and Queenships?"

"What's the point again? Nature always wins."

"We get the picture."

"As long as the picture includes a landscape."

"Gauguin or Van Gogh?"

"Cheese or wine?""

"Ears or toes?"

"No time for a lullaby."

"Debbie Downer meets Dickie Dumber."

He'd plea for the end of misery but wasn't quite sure he wanted it to end, or prepared ready to meet it. I'd rather have the money than the moment. And now, a mind flush begged release. Don't take anything personal. The perpetrator of the harm event directed towards you is a projection of the actor spawned by personal spurns others inflicted. but then note, the victim may take the same approach. Beware. Beware. Retraction can become as deadly in form, force, and spirit as attraction.

A brief interlude required of itself a mind flush in this

Word Melody Letter

I guess it's good I don't need you any longer. I still need the memories, though. They are a general elixir for our traveled time together. Gentle, infuriating, smooth, scarred, in general, essence of life and living itself.

He stood from his chair. Shuffled over to the word processor keyboard, began the music of writing along the keys. The keys betrayed his efforts, at times, or perhaps the betrayal lingered inside his fingertips. No matter. The journey had begun. To begin is the start of anything, of everything.

"Hello, how are you?" he asked the blond-haired person. She had just walked into the company lounge for the dark stuff, coffee, which injected into morning sojourners an ink to infuse purpose in pen clicks, then made something legible of the effort. From out of it a letter, syllable, word, sentence, paragraph. and too, a life together of 33 years trembled to ensue, as yet unknown in scope and size to each of them . . . .

The reader of this moment's literary piece must fill in the blanks as they see fit, from their life perspective. For me, it doesn't have to be perfect. Just done. Lay down a blanket bunch of teardrops and wherever mosquitos roam, they will call it home.

All the best.

The Author

P.S: refreshing. now back to work!

P.P.S.: Ignore the Leaning Tower Of Beer Cans.

On With The Chase

Silence, accompanied by an analytical and ruminative look supplanted laughter, as this group primarily digested science-oriented menus. Their minds probed the etymology of each word, phrase, sentence meaning. Only the fire pit cackled at inopportune times it seemed, as response to audible sounds, as if the joke went over their little sparked floating heads.

"Pound it with a sledge hammer."

"Or a bread stick."

"Wouldn't help."

"These moments are like beach sands. Absorb blows, then morph into other forms . . . of sand mounds."

"Much like humans, humanoids, animal and avian creatures, insects, viruses."

When will this welding end?

"You've overlooked this little portion of the world for so long. I guess we should appreciate you for that circumstance."

"Divorced, after 22 years or so. Married about half of my life."

"What happened, between you, and your beau?"

"She was perking another guy for half our marriage. I found out, in the 20th year."

"Horrible."

"Always thought it odd she didn't want to celebrate our 20th anniversary."

"That's a clue."

"For her it would have been like attending a closed casket funeral."

"One of many clues, like the unusual smells on her dirty clothes. Smells of another man, or perhaps many other men. She settled on one, eventually."

"And now you're here. Poking science for profit."

"And the worst of it. She robbed me blind. Had to start all over again, financially."

"Like I said, poking. We all poke, someone, something, or other."

"No. We are the pork, at one time or another."

"So, this little excursion is the latest barbecue."

"And the cooking aromas are all wrong."

"Not sure I follow."

"Our Master Chef. Somethings off about him, I can smell it."

"Lost his touch?"

"My last meal, this venture. Then off to other things."

"You mean the pay. Your escape avenue."

"One last hurrah."

The sound of an expelled projectile traveled across friction waves, pierced skin, bone, his heart. Shadows fell in his mind, light thinned to gray, then black. He fell beneath the shadows' edge, dead.

Must we all be cursed to like the things that hurt us? Things. What things? Moments. Words. Touches. Actions. Temptations. Retributions. More, but to go on wastes time jewels. Fast receding in glimmer and glow, they pass by our eyes, minds, sights, ruminations. What are these? And Those? Moments rare as the wind blows, random listless madness lipless. Love is the curse, the little weasel.

Fire Pit Dialogue

"Life's about where one wants to insert the didly-doo."

"Didly-don't. Just don't."

"Prick."

"Uncork that whine bottle."

The conversation dragged forward at this point, as each Sorenson's Adventure participant determined a one-upmanship contest might release tension, but perhaps at the point of destroying ever so lightly a comradeship opportunity purpose. Hell, I wasn't even comrades within myself, so a similar type of melody proceeded, at least from my perspective. Narrators rule. Narrators rules, anyway, elite-like.

"Don't go there."

"Time to cut bait."

"Fate demands it."

"A cruel god, that Fate."

"Goddess."

The fire pit spurted an unexpected blast skyward.

"Just in time."

"The pit has spoken."

"If we would only listen."

"Fire flatulence."

"Freak us. We're doomed."

"Oh, I get it. This is one of those times when you can dis me, but I can't dis you."

"Ack bat ayou, ossholea."

The group mindset now became to listen to the pit. Attempt excavation of wisdom in the sounds random of spits, churgles, kindling dances.

The fire pit spoke to them, and the fire pit spoke to him. It seemed the voice heard by them and him rang a different bell tone. Theirs rang loud and clear. His rang softer and more haunting.

Endings Beckoned, But Escapes Ruled

He is rain. He is wind. He is nature itself. He is birth. He is death. He is all and everything else. But no creature or being of this universe could hold such power for long and not become corrupted beyond hope or recognition. It remained as the enticement, those lonely only short moments. And reason to live more, learn more, become more in his native-born world of the ghoul Clan. Poisoned lab rat. Killer, by generational design. Toxic.

And always and sometimes the wind's hidden hands pushed and punched a different path. "What do you want to do with your life?" A question never asked as he grew up. His life journey portrayed itself, in the eyes and voices of the Elders, as a fixed point, a connecting dot in the history of the Clan. Such an upbringing gave purpose, but such purpose lived as a stripped bare slave about to be auctioned at the hitching post.

In the nature of humanoid existence, the first inclinations of course didn't ring loud as an independent one. Rather, the bell rings toned in unison, or like falling dominoes, one after another, without breaks in sound, until completion of the sounding course and community chorus. He wanted for judgment, but despised rule. What to decide remained a maskless tool.

A deviation from the expected course raised the Elder voices, not in praises, but in rebukes. Something new resisted this way traveled, until the new became the accepted, after travails and tribulations many, and reached the eventual destination of old ways and wisdoms, and sometimes, legends of mythic origin, if enough eons raised in height and breadth. A leaf's journey it was, he noticed, during his nature studies. How to navigate the elements, essentially, he learned. The rest of his life, he practiced.

"Teeth. I need teeth," he thought. "And knowledge." Teeth and knowledge could take him far, at least from the perspective of a youngling.

Noted suspicions, he did, that Elders served as levelers emotionally. Even keel cherished. Crooked arrow disdained. Sharp curves cut along the path's edges. Blood spills eventual, gradual, accepted.

He didn't understand why he could still see value in the crooked and broken items, personalities, wisdoms. He hated them, these thoughts. As a curse they increased and became prevalent, yet he learned to accept them as baggage carried along the learning journey; the acceptance journey; the living journey for all things, creatures, beings even down to the bared stones and course rocks. Getting there, getting there, even if along steps unsure.

He lived his life often waiting for the other shoe to drop. The bell ring awaited. As start and at finish. Imagined the sound, and expected the moment of it, but no reverberation in the air readily announced itself. When the full effect of the sound did come, jumbled his mind fluctuation regularity, it did, until ignoring ethereal vibrations no longer remained an option. What to do next marched as presentation dance according to regular brain waves protocol.

"Just forget me, Hon. Just forget me. When you no longer harbor a single memory of me, that's fine with me."

"Why?"

"Because."

Such conversations in his head existed tilted, disturbed. Where did they come from, their origin, sound, syntax of word, sound of voice, he wondered. No one he readily knew, from experience. Meaning eluded him. Thoughts poked through his mind mist.

"The secrets out. Gods can die."

They do, have, in every religion tale. A belief exists they can be reborn. True, they can, but only in the minds of humanoids. Their existence in present, past, or future is irrelevant to all other living, existent, extant biological entities. The mystery of it all continues, until a time uncertain, even in such connective moments as gods themselves may have constructed.

Erased from memory he understood. But die? Gods? For what purpose or pause?

"It's always stupid o'clock somewhere."

Morbid Mind Stuffs

Some in the group plotted to kill Sorenson, basically for the money, and also spurred on by the thought he was leading them to their death.

Aurie found out because his hearing is greatly enhanced, as well as his strength (4 or more times that of normal humanoid as he is more creature than humanoid), so he throws them off his track by allowing himself to seem a true believer in Sorenson which gives the group incentive to kill Aurie to get him out of the way and to remove a Sorenson ally. So, Aurie allows himself to be killed in order to fool the plotters and mentally inject into them an over-confidence and gain a feeling they have weakened Sorenson's ability to carry out his theft of their money promised.

Switching to Aurie first person . . . and . . . go!

Some of my notes were lost along the way of this jovial excursion, from a ghoul's perspective, so I've taken a few liberties jumping back and forth in time scenes, because staying practical during the mission needed such fated nonsense and sensibility interspersed.

So, they killed and buried me, but I wasn't ghoul dead. Just dead from a humanoid's perspective. I can still hear their voices from below ground, feel the vibrations of their physical movements, and worm this body through the rock-hard soil, like putty squeezing in and between various underground frozen fissures to a point where I put myself just below the tent of the suspects, and eventually, come up from underground, suffocate them, and pull them downward, squish them up into soil enrichers, like oatmeal, until their remains blend into the underground world. Helps my biological friends, and my own nutritional needs.

!!! Note, while I'm playing dead, and moving around underground, the soil contents, so rich in proteins and minerals, makes me become a bit crazy wild in thoughts. I guess I should give some examples.

I imagine many ways to kill each of them before actually doing so in the ghoul method of quick and efficient. Then, disposal of the innocent body after the evil and ill mind is extinguished serves as soil enricher and birther of new biological molecular babies.

While slivering around and along underground, I can detect where the victim targets peed or pooped, or walked, or spit, and figure out how long the detritus has been absorbed into the earth topsoil or ice sheet or snow carpet. The freshest of the fresh spots found leads to the victim. I then reach my biology forward and mimic arms and hands upward, clench the target at an available appendage and spin the body like a drill if necessary to navigate the below ground world which is much alive but mostly unseen by above ground dwellers.

I can also track scents and adjustments to the natural soil and underground contents, then decide where animals, creatures, humanoids died, and how long they have been dead. I found evidence of much activity. The area was alive in biological and chemical traces of varied life forms underground. I further met underground creatures in some cavernous openings, essentially worm-like creatures, slithery in movement, and some spider like creatures, and some bat-like creatures as a joy to behold and befriend, chemically and otherwise.

Oops. Wasn't in the least threatened by them as this body of mine fed on such life naturally, dissolved it, as it became hopelessly stuck to my skin, only to become absorbed as energy boosts. Before my timely death, from a mission perspective, I left clues for the pretenders of evil. I knew they plotted to kill me, which served the mission well. I left them signs. Retired early after many of the campfire get-togethers at end of work day. Disappeared during some of the work assignment drills for evidence and knowledge. Made it a point to keep them organized and directed. The murder group upended these efforts at every turn. In other words, they hooked themselves to the bait.

I believe it possible one or more in the murder group orchestrated the crash of the other plane, again, to increase their shares of the pot, after they deduced the plane passengers were useless or a hindrance to their plans. The thief in the murder group also knew big tech techniques to monitor and steal money in the other plane groups on-line bank and equity accounts.

My research assistant in reality worked as an intelligence agent, privately, so she knew all of the same techniques as the murder plot group. In advance I decided the money of the deceased, and the murder group, should be moved to living relatives, except for Sorenson's share, if the mission was completed according to my calculations.

The Master of Boredom

Aurie had learned, during his ghoul learning years, the power of boredom over a humanoid's soul. Many of them just had no stomach for it. Patience in humanoids had long been receding in the gene pool, over generational spans, as the technology world increased in influence. At this point in current time, boredom possessed an effect of increased opportunity to become inflicted by emotional distress and eventual anxiety inflections. A humanoid, or any target of harm or outer body control, would easier succumb to attacks during the boredom affects. But I think it is a planned pause, necessary for recharge of mind and spirit. Even acts unkind to a sentient mind serve purpose as wisdom opportunities.

He had become a Master at boredom inflections. Used it at opportune times to weaken an aggressive transgressor, and even used it against obnoxious in manners allies.

Where he stalked now confused the out and in of him. His imaginary moth kept him alert, darted back and forth, up and down, a winged crusader if ever there was one. Not as horney as the red cardinal outside his morning window, but still plucky.

A full moon or so in time, back at his apartment in conversation with the research assistant, they together play-acted a scene of the remaining Team members seated around a snow and ice scarred investigation site campfire. In the here and now, a similar play commenced amongst the remainder of the Team members. Their voices tickled his ear lobes, pricked the drum skins, echoed from afar and like nearby skeeter buzz all at once. An odd orchestra of sounds persisted in his head.

"Maybe, baby."

"How insulting."

"I know."

"I don't."

"I chose rhyme over chime."

"Politicantations notwithstanding."

"You're hopeless."

"I know. Still looking, though."

"That's a lot of so."

"Broken threads difficult to mend."

"I hear buttons striking the linoleum."

"Too much so, they do."

"On with it then, before this journey ends afore it begins."

"As every journey ensues."

"Your mind transfusions weaken the effort."

"So noted."

"I'd say sew me another thought, but as it is, we are Afghan rug heavy deep in it now."

"I'd want it no other way."

"Pig."

"Pigs are people, too."

"Only in Orwell's world."

"I know that world."

"Nothing else to say."

"Odd we must express such a thought."

Her subsequent silence betrayed a long train running sound, in his mind. At this next moment, he mind remained seated in his apartment accompanied by the research assistant. Iron, steel, chunks, hunks of battered metal, friction worn, yet every silent sound birthed another thought. Silence sometimes had a way silky mysterious in the human-oid mind.

Blackness then blare. Somberness then stare. Dust in the air. Itch in the hair roots. Kicks of the horse boots. The silent rings sucked in a monk's self-torture of non-syllabic thoughts chained against the walls of a mind in static self-flagellation stasis.

"One's self is a cruel master."

"Or mistress."

Silence begged interjection of the moment once more. Then a chorus of voices, of varied genders, insect sounds, day birds and night flocks, creatures alive unhinged, creatures dead as meal service.

"You turn course."

"Moonglow soft."

"South of the border looms."

"Not today."

"Cut's like a knife."

"Bail some hay."

"That's taken as a citified insult."

"Take it or leave."

"Ah. Done."

"You may have the last word, but I'll have the last thought."

Slayed he was now. From even below ground he felt the campfire heat massage the ancient skin pores bestowed to him by his Clan. Forced to move on along the path of the imminent day's journey. His mental feet seemed weighted like ancient Great Lakes boulders, randomly spread across a plain of post glacier aged snow flows.

"Primordial."

"Sometimes you just have to trek across the gravity in an opposite direction."

"Your kind can do that?"

"My kind. Whatever you mean by that verbal spout, sure, okay, sure."

"You mean it doesn't matter."

"Nothing really matters."

"Anyone can see."

"Nothing really matters."

"To you, perhaps. Not me."

"You deviated."

"Deviation intrigues my mind."

"Tickles it, ay?"

"You could think that."

"Oh, pardon my mind."

"Again, I will."

"Coffee time."

"Sips of such an elixir quenches more than thirst."

"More."

"Are we dying, here?"

"Not at all. Only the moments recede."

"Only?"

"Like waves of the breeze."

"Like quakes of the seas."

"The lonely know."

"And some sew so."

"The calm before the coffee."

"Smell it brewing. Hear it pop."

"Ready in just a jiffy."

His skin surface pricked by memories of the research assistant's angelic voice sounds, and punched by her mind waves, he began to re-cover towards a more humanoid sentience status. A curse of the ghoul world while extant physically in the humanoid environment floated as the push and pull between each existence, at times on one side of it, then the other, and sometimes pinched in between each.

"Patience. Too much of a good thing dulls the taste buds."

"The dulcet rings of my taste buds deafens the insides."

"Careful. You may consume yourself. Then where would we be?"

"I fear to tell you."

His assistant reminded him that every transformation from ghoul to humanoid and back involved a complete consummation of each, then regurgitation. Ghoul. Humanoid. Humanoid. Ghoul. An august indigestion experience. Painful, too. She couldn't possibly know he was a ghoul by existence, unless she too lived as ghoul. And she wasn't. At least, he was unable to perceive such existence within her.

Ghouls can achieve existence status in two places at once, but not terribly long in time, and not completely in either. Constraints to such interactions existed. An evolution moment seemed to have presented itself at a not opportune instant. One of these moments commenced at present, the other in the past, as memory. Each moment and memory served purpose in value, sometimes intertwined like sexual partners along the nature scales. He knew well in order to accomplish his mission plan, her help was much needed, as an ally. If she wasn't in fact an ally either as humanoid or ghoul, at least a competent foe could help, as he felt confident he could navigate the trips and pitfalls of such an alliance.

It occurred to him, if she was of ghoul blood and essence, her family befell ostracization generations ago as means for her clan to enter the humanoid world more permanently, to understand it, to deconstruct machinations of it, in near entirety, to learn how to navigate it better, when necessary, as now. Such excommunications sometimes had not occurred due to incompetence, but instead happened because of extreme competence which created fears in the ghoul elite classes. Failure by extreme competence wasn't rare in any culture. It was pretty much the norm. And too improved the culture and purged it of sins and indiscretions. The deserts of history had been littered by the favored incompetent, and so too by the over competent, but in lesser numbers of the latter Clan permutations. Each grouping suffered in purpose. Only in notoriety was the line drawn.

Notoriety could become a curse, over enough of a time passage. As the demon world coveted secrecy and the secrets thereof, either consequence still served notable purpose. Time wasn't necessarily a healer. Sometimes an after-effect involved permanent mutations ugly. Ugly served purpose. Ugly as fungible beauty in mind, body, spirit existed. Eventually all become ugly, in the ground, at least by the humanoid standards.

"Oh, what a beautiful skeleton." He laughed at the thought. In the archeological and anthropological worlds, and too the metaphysical, such a statement merited frequency of pleasant expression, accompanied by a sip of sweet wine dripless, or lip pocked beer swigs.

"And now I must sit and pee," he thought. "Poop complimentary."

"We've thought and talked our way beyond the breakfast path."

"That hurts," he blurted from the toilet room confines.

So now he remained in his apartment. Now existed there, in between the camp fire moments, each interwoven in time path waves.

"We can imagine time stopped and still catch a breakfast bite."

In the creases of time, in two places at once, radiating warm and cold at the appropriate moments in each. Mind blown. A skill he had always admired among the Elders had now been achieved. No time for glory hounding. Mission moments passed near campfire flames and the Sorenson crew. Research assistant seated nearby in his apartment on moment-in-time calls passed as movie frames passed slowly, book pages turned slower.

He could hear the Cratch creature nod in agreement. He thought nod, because even a nod from the Cratch created a noise quite audible, due to the hybrid body components intertwined amidst anatomy. The Cratch existed as a three-creature compliment of crow, rat, roach; four creatures actually, because all three creatures existed amidst the central core anatomy of an earth humanoid transformed by mysterious chemicals. The final mixed transformation appeared as ghoulish in nature, but it wasn't a ghoul. No humanoid born anatomy existed in ghouls. Ghouls could only mimic such an anatomy, as unpleasant as the experience occurred.

"I need a pooh, too!" the research assistant blurted.

"Just a sec. In the later stages now," Aurie responded.

"Wiping stage, I presume," she said, "I'll go outside in the back."

"No wait! The outside back has become commandeered by a wasp clan."

"So be it!"

He shrugged, then shouted, "Beware the ouchies!" Perhaps she was joking him, but then he heard the door open and close. "Damn." He proceeded at the vestiges of last wipes to his posterior emanation's point of exit. After a slight and tilted stance, then a pull on his drawers, and finally a firm push upon the white toilet tank metal lever, his episode ended in this drama. Sprits of water streamed mangily from the almost properly working sink faucet. Two long hand and accompanying digits swipes across a now somewhat rigid towel, abused by overuse since the near ancient time of last laundering and done.

He walked into the living area and found her standing as a wide and bright smile beamed from her face. "Gotcha!"

He moaned. He would have groaned, but a moan escaped of less energy consumption. A competitive nature oozed from her soul. It pleased her much, he could see.

"Almost time to break the fast," she rolled off her tongue, while the flashlight in her right hand, raised high above her head, beamed like the dark background soliloquy moment of a main character in a live theatre production. The arc of the beam enhanced grotesquely her facial features of self-assured exhibited confidence in a mission successfully completed.

"You did. You did." He admired her effort, if not completely her competence quality, yet.

"The eggs are in final boiling stage. Just like you desire them, soft boiled. Easy on the teeth."

His teeth. They sought more texture than a chowder egg soup. But to complain when food is served, a curse dare.

"Sweet and warm caresses of the stomach await my pleasures," he groaned, as compliment to the previous strategic moan.

The sweetest moment of soft-boiled eggs consumption rested on the instance of choice between sucking in the obedient soft yoke and white outer edge, or pressing the teeth completely in and through the compliant texture of the creation in whole. He determined a bit of both necessary, similar to the choices made during an erotic and charged moment of consumed pre-copulation temptations. He preferred use of his hands only, but subjected himself to the humanoid method of crafted metal stokers, spoons, out of respect for her culinary cooking efforts. Also, redundancy ruled in certain humanoid situations, more specifically, during pre-copulation moments and cooking efforts, not to mention the mastication rituals adopted by varied ethnic and demon groups, all as it were, inherited and developed from earlier incarnations along the evolutionary scales in both worlds. Demons and humanoids were in-kind memory hoarders throughout every day of existence, and many times the most common riches of memory could be classified as copulatory or edibility moments and events. These events sometimes lassoed the remembered and casted them into a near trance creating a void between time and space. Such moments were dangerous depending on the physical and mental reality moments party to the memory haunts. Sometimes memory acted like curses.

All of these moments together troubled him, as they had been conjoined together for a bit of a while, so he wondered if his cover as a humanoid resulted in a convincing performance. Her intelligence beamed forth as high-level, a designed choice of his clan leaders, particularly since they were quite familiar of her clan's competencies in this regard. He did wonder whether her clan's numerous generations of existence in the earth realm had watered down her ghoul inherited instincts, washed away by humanoid genes copulation and subsequent birth injections. He resolved to treat her with respect as ghoul, even though he wasn't quite sure her ghoul inheritance still factored into her personality, mentality, and physical attributes and talents.

A Single Ear Hair Irritates Mean

The problem with advanced technology like mobile phones, and desktop computers is the deception. Reality exists outside of these mind-numbing binge instruments, yet, humans and humanoids exist transfixed, hypnotized by the fantasy world these instruments represent. Reality in the real world is the righteous fear. Survival in that world exists primarily as an ugly affair. Humankind has no better assurance of continued air-breathing than any other creature rested upon the planet's surface. Serfs to the Plantagenet hierarchy, humans and humanoids exist, and the hierarchy themselves are accordingly and without prejudice bowed at the hips to the all-powerful and eternally controlling tenets of nature's mystical wrath.

Scientists contend they have all things figured out, but their agreement is mere whim fancy; a subset of their internalized unwillingness to accept defeat at the task of merging truth with understanding. A fake and fraud mentality lurks as a virus residing deep inside their own biology, while they pretend their essence portrays a condition of existence above such natural rules of earth born life viability. Even Einstein knew his membership in the scientific community merely permitted him to play a fool's game. Knowledge didn't reign supreme so much as influence and favor ruled the day. Those who have achieved ruler status begin to degenerate into a conditional state of reality resistance, fevered by death fears either physical, financial, or control lost over engines of their own power, particularly when that reality topples them from the pedestals of vainglorious fame they have ascended into. Intellectual ejaculation is a gift of the famed Holy Spirit. Afterwards, during relax time, the folded and dry boxed tissues beg a taste of the ephemeral magnificence.

"Who said that?"

"Does it matter?"

"Who said what. Only matters if you want to punish someone for their words."

"Or praise them, falsely."

"Or envy the wisdom."

"A difference without a distinction."

"Exactly."

"Perception is everything."

"Perception is puke."

"This merry-go-round ride word salad evokes amusement in me."

"We didn't need to know that."

"You did. Trust me. You did need to know that, exactly."

"Your zipper's down."

"Not as down as yours."

Laughter finally interjected the noise parade. Drips of their virulent juices prevented a frustration of crushing weight.

"Verbal stones can't break my bones, and names will never avert me."

"Someone knock the philosopher."

"Which one?"

"At this oral rate, we'll all be rapping soon."

"In fists or musical emanations?"

"Let's flip on it."

"Flip what?"

Middle fingers raised in praise amongst all. Equal opportunity insults served to weaken the sound offenses filtered into the cold-of-heart wilderness. The environs surrounding and amongst them had already absorbed all physical emanations and motions sent forward as tin soldiers heeding marching orders, not unlike the butter knife spread upon the baked forest canvas, coating it over in the main compass directions with all of their human and humanoid essence. Wilderness calculated the noise and aroma codes more precisely than human and humanoid made plastic and electronic machinations. Every syllabic protrusion of their voices lowered their standing in the food chain of this environment. They rapidly approached worm status. What holds humans back is hidden in an envelope of irrational fear. It is the overdue invoice they fear to open. The repercussions of such failure, to open the seal, only heightens with every action delay.

There is time for rumination; time for sleep; time for calculation; time for weep; but there is no time for inaction. Inaction is death; the shroud rolled over the body; the silence only of overt action. The non-human world still ticks, inside and amidst the body exterior; at all times; to infinity; until infinity is vanquished. Silence is a sound. Heavy, weary, deadly fatal if not approached in a skillful and adept manner. To become quieter than silence is to become immortal.

"We must become gods over ourselves before we can conquer the art of a single step in whatever has been deemed, by choice, to be the absolute proper direction, and still, the destination path may end in failure, or even in a success of failure, yet life goes on."

"Failure brings wisdom, just a bit more potent in the pain reverberations."

"Equally, success is rung by the bell of pains past."

"We can only proceed further if we create a body worn device, either exterior or interior in nature, which provides all the nutrition needs comparable to usual mastication moments."

"I calculate we'd save three to six hours of time per day, including preparation time, which could be used to further advance the mind faculties."

"Some genius should figure out the means and methods of human body introduction for this principle."

"We wouldn't need teeth any longer. Saves energy."

"The jaw lines would shrink dramatically over generational time."

"Biting and chewing would become irrelevant, and the saved energy could be used for other functional purposes."

"Excretion would become streamlined, also saving from excess energy usage."

"If the excretion materials could be converted into edible food product, more physical and mental efficiencies would evolve."

"Our evolution integrity would become preserved, then speeded; sped up."

"Olympian, or should I say, Olympus-like, in titan possibilities."

"Perhaps a next project, you gentle souls."

Nary a hint of sarcasm escaped their voiced minds, as there was none such humor to evoke. Humor had led to solemn and scientific contemplation, an inevitable result when such a group of minds interacted. No great banquets, or food events. Time saved would become the god, knocking off the kitchen table top the antiquated concept that time cannot become saved. Time can be cheat coded, just like a computer's function.

"I spank you for the shared wisdom."

"You're miscued."

"This guy grows on you, doesn't he."

"Like a wart."

"Full of compliments today. Nice."

In the pantheon of life, during phantom moments, trust is everything. Unfortunately, it's a rare jewel, trust, and even rarer, found. The universe is in control of earth machinations. More particularly, a master race runs the universe, determines what type of earth creatures are born and how many, constructing the personality, anatomy, and biology of each creature, from microbiological to humanoid, in advance. Earth is an experimental civilization, studied, probed, tested for varied social construct purposes, as means to ultimately create a perfect union of all creatures great and small. Other constructs existed all around the universe, but are intentionally separated by time and distance as means to preserve the uniqueness of the experiment in each location. Such is the theory of existence propagated in the ghoul world.

"What strums the heart strings can injure or heal, and sometimes both results ensue. The both instance breaks the bow string."

"Fap and hatty is yes bay to reed a wife."

"Fat and happy is no way to seed a life."

"Rid me of your riddles."

"Not my purpose."

"Then, your purpose lurks unknown even to you."

"You're trying to sound cool and it, it's not working."

"Oopsies."

"In the night, after the sun beds down to sleep, into that dark place lives memories of love and love lost. Hold onto them. They evoke penance and beam beauty."

"Don't allow yourself to become cursed by anger. Such feeling wastes energies. Deteriorates soul threads."

Human bodies, eek. They begged too much in attentions for itch, scratch, and patch.

Synopsis of our world, any world from a social perspective sentience, a cleansing is sought. Every planet of humanoids mimics a familiar system, no matter the inhabitant make up. Hierarchy, those who control, make the laws, operate under the moral guise in modern times of following the will of the people. Media, those who promote through varied communication forms such as, in the modern world, electronic, for the sole purpose of controlling the formation of the will in the will of the people commandment, acts as a living life form, but a totalitarian demand in all cases and instances including sneezes and eye glances, they promote. The media essentially acts as foot soldiers for the hierarchy.

Merchants, those who market and sell goods, services, and thought schemes, includes the academic culture from the lowest levels of the education system up to the highest. Aided, they are, by the hierarchy's whims, fancies, desires, wants, as all in the higher categories almost solely are afforded the luxury of wants endless. Needs are assumed cared for amidst their lawless wiles. Consequential power afforded them by inheritance, and daft skills of navigation amidst exclusive admittance to varied influential social circles serves as additional citizen robbed bounty collections.

Everyone else, the people. The people are considered as slaves of all the higher social categories above them. The designated slaves suffer categorization as the least in value, per person, yet they grossly outnumber all of the categories of society above their life grade. In other words, many of them are viewed as expendable, as they will become replaced by procreation acts, and then brain washed clean, cleansed of self-control and the baser instincts of humanoid sensibilities, which is essentially the innate nature of the organized education and academic systems. The people pay for this system of control, from birth to death, in mind, body, spirit, and economic output, which is grossly reduced, methodically, by needs of those who rule above them.

In summary, all of life can be boiled down to a base core in this analytical manner. It has always been this system, since the beginning of human and humanoid time, perpetrated upon the perceived lesser classes of worth as a necessary condition by those who achieved control through bold hook or crook shenanigans, then ruled from monuments high and along the dominion steps thereto through use of regal in sound proclamations, suggestions which changed daily. From the hierarchy of the clans flowed forth a stiff dominance over media, merchants, and everyone else who essentially became transfixed, hypnotized, molded to follow the will of the crowd.

Crow voiced crowds-controlled society at the rulers' behest, despite the fact these pop-up virus voicers didn't perceive or realize they were programmed to promote propaganda pusillanimous. The rulers used words to control in modern times more prevalently and quickly, and if not successful, deemed those who didn't follow along as unlawful despite no laws having been broken, except the unwritten law forbidding stings into the minds of the rulers, most generally, by use of words oral or published in the easily made accessible electronic communication forums which essentially served as government agent controlled monitors of those who agreed and disagreed over the latest prevailing social issues bubbling in the cooking pot. Societies have been degraded of humanoid physical contact in the present and evolved into electronic existences and exigencies.

Influence potential is graded by media camera time, publication of the media cake, and then the consumption level of intensity is graded by the educators, all monitored by electronic means, for either quick disposal in the recycling garbage bin or explosions of thought sprayed across all electronic avenues. In this world, on the computer, press a button, read a story online, and marketers monitor the inquiry, clean it, press it, re-package it and voila, instant access to the needs and desires of the people. The merchants and media control who enters the hierarchy and who becomes tripped into a fall upon the sword. Obsession lurked on a perch of cruel possession.

What has resulted is the rumor mill of the electronic world controls everyone and everything. In essence, humanoids have cannibalized the souls of other humanoids for profit, power, totalitarian control of all things humanoid. What are those things? Everything. Every letter of the alphabet. Every word communicated. Every thought emoted. Every action, both public and private, analyzed, graded, categorized.

Loving something, anything, isn't the be all and end all of existence. It's a gift of fate. Loving someone is a fate only two can agree upon, assisted by the sparked presence of truth. Barring the known absence of truth, not much in societal construct really matters. No contact, no relationship, no acquaintance survives long under such circumstances. A nurture of truthful exchanges helps to cement the bond. The seal breaks, sometimes in small spurts, sometimes like a forced bridge dam, when truth ceases to flow in regular intervals. Character flaws, inbred or acquired along the human journey, influence the intellectual and emotional growth, but almost never defeat it. Growth is oiled by habit, circumstance accepted or defeated depending on the avenue perspective. Is this a path I should tread upon, or one to skip or avoid in advance. Whether city, town, or hovel, while a water gush from below ground which breaches the surface tends to upend all in the vicinity? It's ghoul time again.

No government is ever satisfied. It is a beast of unquenchable hunger and thirst. First it takes your body aided by corporations and like business entities who act no different than war-time paratroopers; then it dispenses and spreads a poison cloud over your mind with the help of media soldiers; and finally, the most precious commodity is pilfered, your soul, aided by police power minions.

Are you kidding?

Truth is a fungible commodity printed with an expiration date. This century is manufactured by Big Tech; works like any industry. Provides product, modifies as needed, not by consumer preference, but by master's / owners. New slavery.

The easiest means for demons of ill intent to defeat all of humanity is to compel at least one humanoid to forgo truth as a rule. Odd exits these humanoid demon configurations allow. Who tortures themselves on visions of torture? Truth is a lie. A lie is truth. Freedom is slavery. Slavery is freedom. We'll get there soon, just don't think. Thinking slows things down.

Self-nuking the brain seemed a humanoid pastime. Truth has been waived forever. Each person who listens to the truth, in any form, either oral or written, will than become compelled to pass on the truth, as a virus of thought, until all communication in any form becomes truthful.

The only hope for all living things is that a pandemic of utter truths alters the minds and souls. Then, a tipping point emerges. Either total and consummate destruction rains down, and any survivors carry on in the same manner, although better, as the survivors can handle truth, like a commodity, a commonality, for which retribution and indignation result in common indulgence, and not uncommon destruction. So that circumstance is it. The solution to all problems societal. Harmony or annihilation. Heaven or hell. The cost is accrued by ultimately making a choice. No! Not that!

Are You Sich Yet?

"You don't know me, truly."

"I can read."

"What?"

"Your mind."

"No. You can't. I would know."

"Well, not so much your mind but your body. The motions, emotions. They are a window to the mind. Signals semaphore."

"Well. I'm exposed. What is my mind wearing now?"

If this moment is about crazy, then consider taking a step back for a moment, because crazy has a short lifespan, must be grasped and consumed before it disappears into the ether. Sure, consider it, but let it die, evaporate, and consider a more sentient day.

It's in times of trouble when we find out who are the real tyrants. In the ghoul world, we sometimes resort to cutting off the tyrant's hand and slapping them in the face with it. It's a symbolic gesture of disdain, as ghouls can reattach their hands, which in a way is good for them, to help remember the insolent nature of tyranny. During the healing process of the grotesque wound, hopefully, the tyrant learns the lesson, as the punitive measures increase in intensity, if not.

The red, single eye, of my night dreams, and eventually, my day dreams attempts communication. I try to speak with it, but the eye becomes angry, as evidenced by the violent visions emanating into my brain. I try to shake the violent visions away; the visions of death, grisly after-effects of violent actions perpetrated by unknowns, horrible faces, twisted bodies, apocalyptic landscapes. Perhaps part of my training. To measure up to extreme circumstances in worlds unknown. Need to relax from first person. I will move out a bit to observe myself. Third person perspective unfolded.

As he grew in age, he learned means to deflect the dreams, at least for a short time, then longer in time, then make them vanish, but they always came back, courtesy of the red eye. Explore his ghoul heritage? Tiring, that effort is.

"How many times can I watch that movie?"

"Until it sticks."

"Shut up already."

Misty Purpose Hop

He was only told he had been summoned. Summoned? From where? For what purpose? The Clan Elders, at least those whom he could remember, always responded to questions about his own origin, advised politely the matter was his to discover, as was the case for his purpose. They were not privy to his purpose, only that each of them, him included, had been created to fulfill a specific destiny while traveling along the Clan etiology chain. Everything's all right. Safe and sound. Around and around. Ease into it. Let it come to you. Catch and grab and avoid the nab, until the right time.

So, he imagined his origins from youth until now, perhaps a genie in a bottle, summoned by someone, either by accident or intent, malevolent or otherwise.

He remembered his own attendance at a carnival, when he was so young, his chin barely cleared the betting table. Checked his pockets for coins, found the appropriate denomination, then placed the coin on a number. A rickety chirp sound emerged from the roll of a large wheel, dotted along the edges by 2 inch or so metal pegs crossed upon and tapped into a bendy metal stake. The impact points emitted a chirp, and the sounds echoed off large tents adjacent and across the dirt path intersected by an endless river row of similar tents.

He reached into his pockets several times, placed a coin onto the same number over and over. The spins became so common in sound to his ears, he could almost not hear any other sounds, including the last wheel spin click. Hypnotized he became to the process. The click guidance gave a simple, and for some gifted of less sentient audible faculties, simplistic view of the journey rules.

The present physical moment again interceded, intruded upon his dream state, pulled him back into the Sorenson mission atmosphere. The mission group's rumination faculties alerted him to a status heightened towards the point of mentally hinged unhinged oratory moments. Nature's aromas grounded him in the specified time moment.

"The elemental law of nature is that nature doesn't care. We've all regressed a few rungs down the dominant species ladder."

"Where are we now?"

"Somewhere near the bottom rung."

"Short version?"

"We are now merely a food source, the only value relevant for the world we are about to enter."

"Refreshing, to know, in a morbid sort of way."

"But do we truly understand?"

"Sounds like a death march."

Only nature tunes played in response to the human and humanoid voiced emanations, not directly, but generally. All noise created by the humans and humanoids schemed relevant to all elements of the forest and tundra environment salad.

"Nature is evolving as a protective means to assimilate our presence."

"Hopefully we will be accepted."

"Right, but not as food."

"Perhaps we should make ourselves unpalatable."

"Perhaps some of us already seem inedible."

"No such thing. All things of this universe are edible."

"Then, the question becomes whether digestible."

"And if so, beneficial, or deadly."

"Errors emitted of some become a generous golden chalice for others."

"Our only value, from nature's perspective. The trees will not bow to us, or move back their long, pointy, furrowed arms. The soil will not smooth a carpet path. The biological essence will not discriminate, except in calculation of edible relevance."

"We exist as an accepted nuisance."

"No. We are potential life-sustaining protein."

"Even upon death."

"Yes, after the post-mortem creatures join the feast."

Further walking, unsteady and untrue in step, interrupted the visceral voice modulations, then silence reigned as the totalitarian nature of it wanted to do, then back to humanoid sounds, for a purpose, and not of fancy origin.

"What's that sound?"

"You mean, unusual to your ears, and not to ours?"

Silence reigned once again, as blockade to ignorance imparted by the many footsteps.

"You all know we are merely trying to fit, in here, in this place. It is the nature of a human psyche."

"And so too a curse."

"Deadly cute."

"Our individual destiny is not so much important, in the grand scheme of this world."

"We serve a purpose or would like to think such."

"Feckless furked, we breathe."

"As turkey vultures circle soar elegantly and peacefully above in wait of that special moment, preceded by a death rattle, when one of us might become a next meal."

"Furk you. Furk me. Furk us. Furk we."

"Shakespeare's jealousy furks a refrain refreshing."

Hush near the brush. Therein lay poignant stings all bunched into one larger surface sting. Tense for the low-lying vine branches as they scrape thin and seep a grin of sharpness upon exposed skin. Better to become struck at a chunky part of the anatomy, but not many times unbearable. Sweeping willow trees desired an avenue, brushed their tresses outward as cunning available caresses provided by the wind engine, and thwacked from delicate looking and long branches upon their exposed humanoid skin areas; announced an effect of red streaks upon escape retraction movements. Chess match in the losing phase.

The worst was the birch. Staunch, solid. The thinner a branch litter of numerous tentacle extensions, the more severe the mind horrors, as many points joined and twisted, lurched intertwined upon impact. A pinch of many needles dug and dug more of jaunty lurks.

All such matters served as prelude to greater threats of energy release, as nearby animals absorbed into their bodies, through smell and sound captures, a preternatural instinct of defense by flee, or attack by physical defense maneuvers. Most of the foliage and fauna terrors resulted in dry redness, small tack sized bumps, skin shredding, all later cured by biological entities microscopically working for the humanoid, but animal strikes might leave permanent damage.

"You covered this in the Training."

"Yes, I did. All of you didn't attend," Aurie cautioned.

"You didn't cover one thing."

"Yes."

"You didn't cover what happens if one of us disappears."

"Cost-benefit analysis."

"Oh. Makes sense."

"Painfully so."

"More food for us, then."

"Yes. More food."

The trek continued unfruitful as brutal time wasting. They headed back, reached camp.

"Ok. Rest time. The next phase begins soon. Refer to your schedule programs for assignments. Each of you should know it, as long as the program was previously reviewed."

"Right. Double blind study. Each of us works in two areas of our expertise."

"In the event of a situation that becomes unable to report."

"That's a very clinical way to state one of us goes missing."

"Hazard pay has been factored into your contracts."

"Sure. Sure. That takes care of it."

"Just a quick tip. If anyone goes missing or becomes incapacitated, the odds of the remainder surviving the journey decreases."

"Yes, and continues to decrease if more encounter tragedy."

"Remainders?"

"Tragedy?"

"Like getting eaten."

Some loud laughs betrayed the depths of their separation from usual civilization niceties; some quieter chuckles choked forth like soft cymbal stick taps. Some silence ensued as a tasked symphony yet to become completed in composition. On the cusp of a finale uncertain stage progressed. Up, down, up, down, slow, fast, certain, strange, expected, neglected. The music never changed. Certainty along the tundra only existed in an irregularity of unexpected motions.

"Is that situation the reason you never state our name?"

"Sure. Mission first and foremost. Socialization is only recorded to complete the task at hand."

"Communal socialization. How about that type."

"At the nightly campfire, if necessary."

"The campfire or the socialization."

"Nature never rests. Never. It is the death of many a humanoid in this type of environment."

Looks of non-emoted plaster-stiff stares were exchanged as visible conversation, then each face ephemerally cracked into tiny pieces. He didn't need stares to identify. He distinguished a team member by their aroma, and from great distances. This circumstance somewhat annoyed him; served as necessary curse of his species.

"Rest, for now."

"In peace, I shall."

Sarcastic laughter ended the verbal serenade. Second violin needed some tuning. Their rest time, now. His rest time never entered into the equation. A mind massage awaited cranial attention.

He's not the government's stooge. Bitches, bastards, gender bend-ers. Mere distractions along the road to a better humanoid existence, he supposed. Those kinds of distractions served as civilization killers. The food didn't grow itself into palatable delights. Craft and technique needed to create edibility, in the humanoid realm. No matter the choice, the humanoid element intruded. Crickets preached loud in the alley of his mind. His ability to detect and dissect their brain thought rhythms unmasked how many sick furks inhabited this assignment.

"How does a ghoul survive so long?" He wondered. Genealogy, in-corporated into his familial ranks in the demon plain of his origin ruled. He could incorporate the damage done to his body by absorption of the weapon elements extant, then converted it into a strength, as his mind and body evolved based on trauma events.

Is the universe a mere atom among many other atoms? Or more like a random storm infecting random planets, planetoids, solar systems? We're all refugees from our own destiny.

"When you believe the world around you looks like a silken web, then the living creatures within it all appear to look like spiders."

He could remember their faces, of the women he had loved, or made love to in yearned desperation to quell insatiable needs forever unsatisfied for one, another, or himself only. Most of their names he remembered, but not all, and for that circumstance of betrayed memory he felt bad, as he still recalled their beauty and passion, but loss of the name stung as much as loss of that high school letterman's jacket, or special and lucky coin, or edge wrinkled photograph, or corner pressed baseball card, or torn page comic book. One day, when proper and specific words of voice no longer sparked from the brain's synapses, he would moan deep inside due to aged frustration. To lose the gift of communication meant a true fall into darkness. He almost felt humanoid.

His mind furked out some brain wave crumbs. Like the time when neither he nor anyone else nearby could or would lift the shade to allow one more glimpse of that nearest star, the one eyeball biting bright, yet so juicy in size, and beam, and light, in the time when no edibles deserved a bite as they would not reward his buds of taste, and no sip of coffee could do the trick of pinching sweet the sides of his forehead. Sounds inside his skull pounded harder and louder than those without.

A poem composed in his youth, he recalled.

"boxed moments, to feel sun rays but not heat waves, to see stars shine but not black of night, to walk the smooth path but not risk the fall's wrath, to hug another creature of two legs or four, these are yearning every moment stores, until time coalesces into serene water shores."

Relaxation achieved.

Mind Rants Continued

Burdens of secrets weighed heavy upon his mind. The journey steps felt steeper. Trips involved. Skin scratches, cuts, tears and rips.

I'm now back in my humble city abode amongst familiar creature friends, and her, too, moving along the twisty tedious path of bated movement.

"I've lost my patience," he moaned. She looked at his face, demeanor. Judged a snark parry begged response.

"Maybe someone will find it and return it to you."

He looked down at her crotch which begged a view. He noticed between her legs, at the precipice of her loins, the outline of a mousetrap.

"What's that," then he pointed with his eyes cast directly upon her loins conundrum.

"Insurance."

He thought for a sec. Didn't want to make her feel uneasy, plus, he needed her help for his mission journey.

"Interesting." A further word excursion begged a tempt.

"Want to see it? How it works?" She began a movement of her arms and hands inward and downward as preparation to roll down the jogging pants which lay baggy upon her lower body.

"No, no. That's okay. I trust your judgment."

"Still?" She anticipated the question exuded by his facial expression.

"I hope you've tested it for effectiveness."

"Many times. Made some adjustments along the way."

He turned around towards the window, then rubbed his groin area, to alleviate the pain imagined there. Wondered how many eunuchs existed out there, in the seedier parts of his neighborhood, as victims of her high-capacity self-preservation methods.

"I could tell you stories, but you could like guess them."

"Sure. Unfortunately. They flood my mind now, red in color, screeched out in voice like a horney male fox."

"You're funny," she said, since a two-syllable laugh pop merited an effort a bit too much of a guttural movement.

"These dialogues, er, our small conversations, are quite enlightening."

"More light doesn't necessarily elicit more truth. Come on, look here."

He awaited a solemn mind silence, but to no avail, then turned around, looked her in the eyes, allowed his gaze to graze the lower landscape of her anatomy. His eyes widened into cue ball size.

"Gotcha!"

"You're funny, too," he said, confused at the length and breadth of her wit. The object between her legs was indeed a mousetrap, but it wasn't baited or set properly. The spring, or essentially the silver bullet of the device, didn't exist. She seemed more like a night creature than a humanoid. Filed it amongst other brain matters in his "to be determined" category.

"What we think we see is sometimes more dangerous than what is actually there."

"Threatening, indeed."

"Denial of truth, because many refuse to claim kinship to a view they won't appreciate, grows regularly as mold in the stew."

"You need to recall your schooling."

"How so?"

"The key to understanding governments comes in the epiphany they don't dispense helpful information so much as dispense control propaganda, then keep the helpful info gems and sell to their highest bidding benefactors."

"So then, my paranoia isn't an illness."

"Let's just call it proper, as in proper paranoia."

"That reminds me. I wanted to ask you something."

Something.

Mission Creeped On

Mission accomplished as darkness fell hard like a heavy ocean wave crashed upon a somber beachhead. Sound loud. Sight invisible. What life held still and tight, as a sand pebble in the hand of destiny, remained to be determined.

A thin shroud of fog began methodical a descent upon the land in the reverent manner it desired, for to proceed unimpeded by any extant air of existential reason or rhythm. The unquiet rung as a charmed bell. Many cities and towns and villages of creatures had pre-determined another testy unfurl of daybreak merited a look, for now. The only impediment presently toned as the flea's sting and dogs bark of time passage.

His instincts told him a fogger resided out there somewhere in or on or secreted away in one of the mutants dotting these desolate plains. It can hide in the fog, blend in, because the fur on the creature attracts and refracts light in ways that allows it to become masked among the beamed reflections in the fog.

Ghouls can tell by smell that a fogger is also of partial ghoul blood, so they get along, by nature, if not by pre-disposed Clan treaties or mutually inclusive necessities. Ghouls used markers to traverse land territory. In a tundra land region, mineral markers served as road signs. If an outsider came in and started digging them up, the locals, that is, the foggers, would lose a survival means to remain oriented between point A and point B on any hunt or travel excursion. Sorenson's invasion of this terrain risked the foggers' lives. Still not sure whether Sorenson came here to poach for the mineral or a fogger or both. Each could serve his selfish designed wealth and fame purposes.

The minerals held much potential as an energy source transformable into products needed to power villages, cities, nations. The usual humanoid tack also involved transforming energy sources into weapons systems. In the creature world, generally, such resources served as means to survive, find food sources, protect needed land for such purposes, in other words, further existence of the species. In humanoid circles, weapons served as defense measures, equalizers in the subsistence vein, but in vile hands, as subjugation tools. Just another day in the virus war world.

He remembered advice from Clan Elders.

"Perfection is a smudge that can never become cleaned enough to make it disappear."

They didn't like his retort to such a thought.

"If perfection was as normal as breathable air, we'd all be suffocating on the boredom."

Moment Interruptus

His mind reverted to a research assistant accompaniment past moment.

"I can't help but wonder if I've been receiving communications from an away being."

"Away being? You mean someone not here?"

"No. I mean someone not anywhere, as in off planet, off universe, or off dimension."

"You mean that eye you've talked about, out loud, while dreaming?"

"What?"

"Yeah. You talk in your sleep."

"Oh crap."

He had to look around. Wondered if he was talking to himself or if someone nearby. He didn't sense anyone nearby.

"Do you see it frequently?"

"No. Only in dreams, either day or night."

"Perhaps in quiet moments?

"Yes. That situation seems to be the pattern."

"Does it have a voice?"

"No. No mouth. Just an eye."

"You hear thoughts, then."

"Thoughts. Yes."

"Do these thoughts involve instructions, to do things?

"No. Merely ruminations of circumstances, and potential outcomes."

"Sounds like a road map. You get to choose the direction of travel."

"Once the direction led me right off a cliff."

"Did you die?"

"No. I learned I could fly, in the dream, that is. Fly during the dream, I mean."

"You had me going there, for a bit."

"Sorry. Seems every journey ends in a destination or a death, potentially."

"That's life."

"You left out 'get over it', didn't you."

A silence ensued, of necessity, as his stomach managed a twisted growl.

"I did."

She puckered her lips, as she had often done during contemplation of some semblance search for the final word. He then realized either his research assistant existed near him in real time, or his mind jogged a memory his way.

"I'm waiting," he said, anticipating the penultimate counsel.

"Worry many times is a waste of time."

"Sure." And next would burst forth her final counsel, at least for this extant session of commiseration.

" A moment of final push on the cusp of a last splotched bowel movement."

Extended moments of silence flushed away their conversation detritus. He couldn't help but wonder whether all of these communications happened by movement of lips, or inflections of mind.

"The things I might do are better left to the imagination."

"The things I might imagine are better left undone."

"Sometimes things left undone are best buried in the grave of imagination."

"Unattended to."

"Weeded careless, of no heart tones."

"Instrumental strings pulled so far, ready to break, yet one more pluck calls for sound sustenance."

"The humanoid mind, perhaps animal, too, yearns for stimulation, from nearly any source."

"A galliwogs cakewalk."

"Sweet and deep."

Vocal silence huffed a wicked course. Then again, in a blanker moment. And once more, the empty wordless seconds approached an infinity cycle.

"No words uttered can create quite a racket in the mind."

"And echoes starved for a side of harmony."

"Knock."

"I don't recognize that voice."

"It wasn't a voice."

"A crack of a tree branch, bowing from the weight of cold air."

"Or drawn upon the clenched fist around a thick twig, plunked across a tree trunk."

"Yeti."

The imagined presence of the research assistant transformed into a presence among the team members. Their voices entered into a sound dance.

"There are many gods."

A new topic of discussion then washed upon the dry caverns of their minds.

"The god of no name."

"He eventually allowed a name."

"The god of no face."

"Who has a name."

"The god called God."

"Who sent his only son to die on this desolate planet."

"The son was re-born."

"Yes. And his face is everywhere."

"Great marketing tactic."

"The god who sent an underling Angel to provide a pretty book."

"Made of gold, it was, I think."

"Yes. That made it seem legit."

"Exist many books to proclaim these gods and rules."

"Grisly death chronicles they seem, all in all."

"And the underling humanoids fight to the death over which god is number one."

"You forgot the gods of war implements. The ones who can destroy whole cities with light beams or some such weapon."

"Seems the underling humans and humanoids have copied their works. We can do that now, destroy whole cities on a flimsy flipped queue of words."

"Don't forget the god-like underlings, such as demi-gods, of god blood, who wreak havoc amidst the humanoid biological entities."

"Like a football match in progress."

He shook his head. Tried to zone in on the present moment, scatter the memory haunts.

The fire pit created in the middle of the group seemed to pay attention to the colloquial banter of their mouth utterances. It raised up some red steams skyward; spat red and yellow sparks from the wood chips engulfed. Signs and interpretations thereof rolled around in the heads of the seated viewers who yet attempted to verify whether their own physical status existed as predator or prey in these moments; in these tasks of action for which they would be compensated, in monetary currency.

"I would guess the demons calculate the betting odds, and reap much in monetary rewards."

"You mean souls rewards."

"Souls are currency, pure and simple."

"Ha, Ha! Good one. Sure, these gods are competing amongst each other to collect the most souls, the most currency."

"Someone gave me a soul, and the ransom is my body."

"The body is merely a satchel."

The center fire began a slow fade, then spurted forth some further sparks of life, as if entrance into the conversation sea had been invited. A night wind helped, blew soft but strong enough to cajole further pit action.

"And the human athletes play the game, much like a football match."

"Every now and then a no-holds-barred death match is funded, stoked, for entertainment of the masses."

"And the ones who survive become demi-gods."

"Stadiums rise and fall, all around the world, to host these matches, all to remind the human and humanoid souls about their purpose."

"And what is their purpose?"

"Entertainment for the gods."

"That explanation sounds like misery loves company."

Barcarolle, The Fire

The fire, at the central point of the seated group, spat flames and heated-red sparks high into the sky; sounded cracks and spits into their earholes.

"Seems we became items on the environment menu as soon as we arrived here."

"Appetizers or main course?"

"Does it matter?"

"I much prefer the innocuous life."

"Mister Bland?"

"Indubitably."

"Self-deceit is the greatest lie."

"Who inflicted this philosophy curse upon you?

"I Kant recall."

"I hear a Russell amidst the bushes."

"My Plato is clean. Next course?"

"Have you tried the Camus kumquats?"

"A Santayana wine goes good with that."

"Certainly, would hit the Marx."

"I'm getting food drunk. Time to retire to the Beauvoir."

"I've got a Tillich."

"Scratch it."

"No Butler's here really sucks."

"Scratch that Nietzsche, or it will never go away."

"Far away is where I ass Hume you mean."

"I need a Rousseau sit-down moment. Be right back."

"Be careful. The last person to Spinoza never returned."

"And don't get too Rand out there."

"No Locke for the outdoor latrines here."

"Darn. Out of butter and jam and still one Nagel remains."

"Dewey all retire now?"

"Arendt there more forks? We need more forks."

"I've been itching this Chomsky for a while and still no comfort."

"Another Aristotle of Guinness, please."

"Turing in a Tesla will get you killed."

"Camus back soon. We haven't much time left."

"What was that noise?"

"Sounds like Diogenes hurling."

"I could really use some Bacon."

"A Thoreau recon is sorely needed."

"I hear Jaspers in the trees."

"Please, and surely we are built of Stirner stuff."

"Perhaps the creatures of this place are better Singers than us."

"You Nozick."

"That's a Hobbes homer on the last at bat."

"You're James-in on me now."

"I'm Confucius."

"This whole mess is your Foucault."

"The Unamuno will be rising soon."

"Wollstonecraft won't save us."

"You Buber. Get a grip."

"Tzu never understand."

"Aurelius? Get serious."

"E Nussbaum!. There's wisdom in silence."

"And Death."

"There's a Machiavelli in the woods."

"Nozick knows."

"And now we know."

"I need a glass of Aquinas."

"The Weil is dry."

The search for truth is a fool's game. If there existed a mystical book for humanoids to learn about life, lessons, and to act accordingly, that book probably existed more in effect and usage as a grimoire. It would serve to be used by the humanoids for good and ill, but along the experience path of use, the humanoids and those beings and creatures touched by their presence would also find through experience, counter to many of the grimoire teachings, a broken web of deceit threads, lost souls among the web's detritus, and spoiled dream remnants. There's always someone around who lives willing to make you the fool. Always. The rulers, those chosen and unchosen, are always of a tyrannical mind, as their power can be used to bend the will of the beings who oppose them in perspective, sentience, or otherwise.

Here, There, Everywhere

"Just look around you", Aurie thought to himself, then shook his head to alleviate the lurk hooks in his mind. The truth, in some patch-work form, is likely lurking nearby, despite the efforts of the thought stealers hired by the rulers. We can ignore the rulers until the sting of oppression becomes too agonizing, and many still exist in a status much beyond that point.

Where was I? Heard a voice. Sniffed the air. My research assistant is near.

"What is it?" She asked, adding a confused look.

He sniffed the air again, tried to identify the origin point. He looked around her, and about her, from top to bottom, side to side.

"That smell, aroma, as it were," he remarked.

She glanced him an uncertain look.

"Are you wearing perfume?"

She noticeably tried to not look uncomfortable.

"No. Not usually, not now."

He moved a bit closer towards her, just a few steps. Directed a question towards her.

"Perhaps your laundry detergent, then?"

She pulled the curved neck area of her shirt away from her skin, then lowered her head and sniffed.

"Just me."

Irritated, she grabbed her crotch. Pulled upwards on it a bit. Smiled.

"No pees in a while either." He didn't reflect a laugh, or at least issue forth an uncomfortable smirk, seemed in a bit of a deep and calculated contemplation moment.

"I'm sorry. Just a bit worried. Don't want you to be noticed, out in public, by anyone who might try to insert themselves in our work business."

"I can take care of myself."

See Saw Teeters

His mind ricocheted again, back to what he perceived as present moment time, as the campfire circle re-emerged.

"What was that we just encountered?"

"Smelled like a male."

"I thought female."

"Why does that matter? Could have been an either or neither person."

"What does any of that matter?"

The reporter, Aurie, says he has to relieve himself, a wet one. He walks off, as the others wait. Then sounds in the woods erupt, but he can still hear the campfire team banter.

"A scream?"

"A howl, like a fox"

"A growl, like a wolf."

One of them spouts, "I'll check", and goes in direction of Aurie, fades into the forest.

A few minutes later, Aurie comes back.

"All right, done."

"Wait, where's Benedict?"

"What?" Aurie asks.

"You didn't see him? He went looking for you. We heard sounds."

"Got worried," another says.

"It's the forest. I heard nothing unusual," Aurie says.

"Settle down. We have to find Benedict."

"You didn't see him? He went looking for you."

"Or your dick," another says.

Laughter, some uncomfortable.

"Odd that someone is missing already, this soon into the excursion."

"Soon? This entire affair has been a short walk on a long pier rotted. Each step portents a fall."

"Benedict can be a bit of a prankster."

"Maybe the pranks on him, and it's pay-up time."

"A little bit longer than never is a good bit of time."

"Or a little bit further than almost there."

"Keep up this banter, and we'll be discussing our favorite beer."

"Or arguing about it."

"Arm-wrestling on it."

"What, no wine tasting?"

"What's your favorite steak type?"

"Steak isn't a type."

"Sure, it is, like pork portions. High on the hog, or rind."

Too many trudges longer had tired the spirits, and discussion thereof.

"Benedict still missing."

"Something doesn't smell right."

"I got you there."

"No. I mean the air aroma."

"Like a horse just keeled over and died, then expelled bowel detritus from the hind quarters."

"Not good."

"Something's dead."

"It's a game of hopscotch."

"Watch out for the line shapes."

"A game without the hops."

"Or the scotch."

"Damn. We back on the drinking binge talk again?"

"Anyone notice the lady hasn't offered any sound to this word buzzing crapola?"

"She has a point."

"And a way with words."

"You mean away."

"No words mean a lot. Really."

"Approaching Sanity point."

"In three, two, one."

"Where'd that funky smell go?"

"The way of the world. Listen."

"Sounds like a library out there."

"And near as silent."

The lady makes a verbal offer to this horrid male word salad.

"Time to check out those books, gentlemen, or leave."

"She has a point."

Then the lady zeros in.

"That horse rind smell, and that forest devoid of sound, can only mean one thing."

The males remain silent. Perhaps they know the answer, the conclusion.

"We have found Death's Door."

"Death's door?" one of the men asks.

"Yes, the name of this place."

The men do the grunting expected to shoo away the essence of death.

"Okay, we need a volunteer to knock, or ring the bell, or give a shout, if we are to enter."

A bit of uncomfortable joviality sounded slowly, and unnervingly pricked the atmosphere around them.

Ways And Means

Life is like a human floating in the ocean. You can't see a lot about it, except the immediate surface, and to see further, upward, requires a battle against the sun, water spray, waves, seagulls and more dropping detritus of varied types, and then below, in the unseen, known but not to you, there are predators of all types, as those in the sky, each in their own way trying to survive, like you, on the surface edge.

Look up, look down, get below the surface and look further, but there are no guarantees written or spoken into these efforts. Death teeters from thousands of sources, ready to strike, to grab, to smother, to crush, to sting, to melt you.

Pretty much sucks on the surface, but there are many avenues to pursue for safety. Float, swim, call out to nearby humanoids, and hope they are not of nefarious mindsets. Some are no better than animals seeking to serve their base needs, as they've not evolved into a more sentient being, for whatever meaning or purpose, and some have evolved immensely, but dabble in the acts of inhuman nature.

You wish you could evolve into exterminator, garbage cleaner, of these horrors, but not so in the tarot cards. Still, they are just cards, interpreted by a human, who's purpose and goal is entirely unknown to you. Yes, there are innocent mistakes flowing back and forth. A forgiveness mind helps in those situations, or at least, for some time after.

Everyone is being programmed, to avoid life during entry into the New World of games, entertainment, which allows ignorance of the arrival of a new life form. To live blind in the light is to give strength to the night. The night had become hungry. Very hungry.

Enlightenment

Life existed in the nuances of moments. Many nuances lurked ignored, pushed aside like yesterday's yellowed newspapers, yet these nuances lurked as deadly reminders of the cliff's edge masked in a foliage overgrown. Safe footing existed just centimeters away from certain death falls. Stability rested upon grains of sand. She appeared in presence as just too good to be true, and that's exactly how it turned out, but not unexpectedly. The judge is not exempt from the rituals of the legal system. The most reliable quality you can expect of a humanoid is they will lie to you.

A dank smell pinched up Aurie's nostrils amidst quiet wind calm. The lack of wind failed to betray an origin stench source. Another solace seeking moment invaded for attention. Early morning sounds entered from the bedroom window. He rolled over towards her to find the bed empty, except for impression of where her body and limbs had rested. She was gone. His mind, like clockwork, had wandered from the troupe's campfire barnacle knocks and into memories of the recent past during his time with the research assistant.

He focused on a sound nearby, farther away than the chirping morn birds. A swish and more swishes. A light line, straight, then peeling back emanated from the far wall. The bathroom door was slightly open.

He sat up on the edge of the bed, stared at the floor to separate the carpet from the clothing dropped in the previous night and pre-dawn early morning hours. A walk path existed to avoid detritus of rolled and splayed undergarments. In the crooked display of cloth, he noticed his underwear pants, unrolled them, put them on, made way over to the door, slowly pushed it open. Steam blankets floated under the ceiling. Steam glossed the shower area sliding doors. A high-pitched hum buzzed about his inner ear cavity. Hypnotic it was in tone and rhythm. A light air then caressed his neck from behind.

Such stimulations reminded of a funny story, so he proceeded to orate from the tiled bathroom floor as light entertainment for his shower guest.

"You haven't lived until you've opened a box of cornflakes and noticed near about a third of the way down into it, seated on top of the lonely flakes, is perched a roach, glad to have shared in the breakfast bounty."

"What would you do next?"

"Depends."

"Depends? On what?"

"On whether I move the friend out of the way, or spill it into the sink, watch it scamper, as I turn on the garbage disposal switch."

"Oh no you didn't."

"No. I didn't."

"What is that noise?"

"The neighbor."

The shower water flow ceased, and the shower window glided open. She moved over to the side window, looked out through the glass, then gazed down towards the sound origin. He noticed her pants tighten along the curve of her buttocks, while wondering why she wore pants in the shower. Tingles tickled the inner recesses of his brain, in places not quite yet familiar to this place where his feet were currently planted firm. He had taken many steps upon these tile floors, and never experienced such tingles.

"Oh," she said.

"Sounds like he's dragging another garbage bag. I could speculate out loud about the bag's contents, but it may alarm you."

"Your speculation or the bag's contents?"

He didn't respond, which acted as response enough.

"Scary," she mused aloud.

She turned back to the door, breezed past him while simultaneously grabbing a towel from the door side rack, went back to a couch seat which still displayed a round indenture of her previous visit's taught buttocks print. As she lowered her hip's frame to perfectly plant back into the buttocks print, his voice offered counsel.

"Scary? That's not scary. Scary is watching a spider creep on spindly legs across an object, twig, wall corner, bed cover, then you glance away just for a moment, then retrace your gaze back towards the spider point, and notice it is no longer there."

"Where is it, then?" She asked.

"Anywhere, everywhere, in the tiny crevice, a space perhaps least suspected."

We all have a vibe that, once tapped, brings life to our insides. Eruption corruption, perhaps, it is. When an old Slavic woman tells you "don't get on the plane", then don't get on the plane. Those passengers in the plane, soon alerted by oncoming passengers of the Slavic woman's counsel, play a game to lighten the burden of anxiety. Well, you've got two choices. You can get the furk out, or you can die.

She asked him, "If you had to choose among two emotions, fear or sadness, which would it be?"

Aurie responded, "Fear."

They laughed and piped up, each with a negative jibe.

She responded, "I've known deep sadness. Deep."

Aurie said, "feel free to share". She proceeded to tell a story.

Due to no more money to take care of her cats, Liz and Meg, she had to take them to the Vet. She recounted the injection of the death serum that put them to sleep. She was allowed to pet them until their last breath. The Vet's understanding nature comforted her. She thank him for his assistance, but the sadness in her face hung heavy upon the brow, wrinkled and shriveled, while wetness pockets around each broke into threads like a pants pocket. She strained to hold back the tears as she left the room, walked across the main foyer, and out the front glass doors. Each step towards the car, the sound of each scrape upon the blacktop driveway, shredded away pieces of her heart like the grating of a rectangular block of cheese. Once at her car, which no longer seemed important to her, she realized she saved the car and not her pet friends.

The car had helped her travel through and upon the sharp stones of troubled times. But so too had Liz and Meg done the same, boosted her emotionally. The anxiety in her heart pulled hard in the gut but if felt like it had been ripped from inside, at the intestines.

She opened the driver's side door, squatted and plopped into the driver's seat, placed forearms and hands upon the top portion of the steering wheel to brace upon as pillow for a strained forehead. She couldn't hold back the breaking of the emotional dam. These moments haunted her for very long time periods, eventually eroding away much capacity to feel the pangs and longings of emotions of any sort. Shredded she had become from the realities of life, always forcing herself to cling onto the sentience rope upon which required a firm grip, at the hands, arms, legs and feet.

She could not escape the long fall from the moments at the Vet's office. Her mind swung back and forth between the realm of reality and the realm of escape fantasy.

Now Aurie's tone entered into an attempt to stem the speed of her emotional fall. An uncomfortable sound stage void buzzed as his audience of one awaited alliterations and expectorations from the shadows. He knew the strengths and weaknesses of his gene pool. He was reluctant to pass them on to another generation, until he met her.

He shared some names his family used for pets which seemed to imprint upon the time period of ghoul family history. Penelope, Sabby, Ducky, Tigger, Biscuit, Zuzu, Roy, June, Sunny, Shadow, Danny, Roxy. In their pee and poop and puke stains on throw rugs, wall to wall carpets, faux wood kitchen tiles, bed linens, blankets, pillows, chairs and sofas, rested memories absorbed by the hands holding paper towels and vacuum cleaner hoses and plastic buckets for certification.

She spied an oval shaped black bug, about quarter sized. It swished delicately two needle thin antennae about, carefully reading air currents. Six toothpick thin legs glided the body along in a long and smooth wave of beige colored drywall.

"Ralph!" Aurie shouted, a bit high in pitch, stopped the water bug on a dime. "Good to see you buddy." Aurie stood and scurried in steps to the kitchenette cabinet to pick through worn boxes of chips in varied shapes and textures. "Your feast of crumbs awaits," he shouted, while rushing back to deliver the food.

On The Morrows

Morose grows from the seed planted in a forsaken place, whether deranged city, dank town, or drenched field. Dangled they did, the wanky blooms sprouted from sinewy vines and crooked bark spines. Doom dormant it slayed under moon lights and evening sprites, until sensible loomed chaos magic. Tragic and torn, laid bare the born.

The pee bugle boomed reveille. His search for himself beckoned. He remembered how he knew the research assistant. The smell of her was well disguised, the love smell pricked his brain, where the sensation stored itself deep, for further review. All these years later in ghoul time, and the sensation reactivated, finally, in a vigor fury he hadn't experienced since youth combat training. He imagined the courtship rules, as he observed them as a child, and in another rival Clan, remembered her scent, and the blatant imprint of her facial features and eyes. In their later years of latent youth, on the cusp of adult times, he spied her essence and face again, during another generational courtship ritual event. He knew that she could see him. He stood more stout, chest out, shoulders spread wide, presented himself as a soldier and scholar in appearance, but still he wasn't aware whether his scent stimulated similar feelings in her being and spirit.

Accidentally they bumped into each other, when his thoughts of her had escaped a firm mental grasp, but for reasons unknown to him, her reaction bore a hostile response and posture defensive. Anger seethed deep from within her, sprang forth sharp various joints and anatomy points in her apparition form, points he recognized as combat ready mode, points that could slay him or at least severely wound. The lock of their eyes remained taught, as their limbs flexed in muscular readiness, then she seemed to sense another presence near.

He had fragmented in two, less visible in definition attributable to each fragment figure, and he floated up behind and touched her shoulder blade. She turned and extended violent an arm to slash the being invading her space as flames broke forth from her dark heart swollen rife inside. But he had readied himself, blocked with his chest the short conflagration burst, embraced her for to weaken the blow, but still she escaped and rang out a physical thrust true. Parts of his shadow form became splayed and frayed towards the night beams shaking down from the moon.

Then she fled. He healed in flesh, but stored the broken memory moment. All of this time it scratched and clawed to ring his passion bell, yet he ignored it for mission completion success.

Current Impact

Upon morning's glow, the remainders of the Sorenson team trudged towards their mountain destination point. How much time had passed, none calculated, as if not necessary. Then the leader, Sorenson, always in the front, always the beacon of the destination point, turned and faced the group. Drifting and random voices lowered in tone until silence reigned. Aurie could hear all of these events and sounds from the cave recesses.

"We are here," Sorenson announced to the group which remained alive.

The group of remaining followers looked around. One asked, "Where is here?"

"The entrance." Sorenson responded.

Another strained out, also amazed, "A riddle, it appears, you have spouted at us."

Sorenson remained confident and reassured them in hushed tones. "Listen to the wind. It fades, it dies, in pitch, in sound."

Still a disturbance caused evasion of discovery efforts towards the next point. One of them started to walk. His footprint pads into the snow surface, previously undisturbed in presence, splashed snow detritus forwards with every lifted leg, and sideways in each direction once the foot had replanted towards the earth's natural surface.

The woman, the most observant of nuances details, chimed in. "Wait."

The disturber didn't wait and continued an awkward trudge as snow clumps retreated from his boot's bottom surface.

The woman persisted. "Someone else, or something else has been here already."

"Perhaps still here," the disturber muttered.

Sorenson merely observed, as he could hear his groups observations both oral and physical as their gear rattled from the moorings of the body of each.

"Continue, in your analysis," he directed to no one in particular.

They moved closer, a few at a time, to the footprints planted in the snow surface by the snow carpet trekker. At the bottom of each print could be seen another print, or part of one.

"Whatever has been or still is here, it isn't wearing any foot covering."

The woman expert in tracking then moved forward, exasperated by displaced curiosity of others who could not reach a steady conclusion.

She only used one of her senses, vision. The others she seemed to neglect as irrelevant. She stooped at the cross-print of the first man and the as yet unknown other living thing. She looked more closely, then slowly raised her body upwards for a more distant perspective, then she backed away, then walked around the scene main point. A nasal sniff she exerted, softly, then more in force. She turned around in a circle and seemed to focus on one point, but discarded a stopping point, then retraced her circular motion until like a radar system, pinpointed the unnatural disturbance in the terrain.

"It was here, then moved to there, then back to here, then to there again."

Aurie continued to listen.

"This 'there' you point us towards is nothing but a wall of snow, laying against a mound of dirt."

"Yes," she agreed. "A 15 feet high mound of dirt, and 6 feet wide in some places."

"What are you saying?"

"Whatever walked, or more like glided from here," she pointed to the ground, "continued onward towards the mound, where it disappeared, or perhaps entered."

"These footprint sizes reveals anatomically a creature of over 8 feet in height."

"And an injured or deformed leg. See the drag lines on the right foot."

Sorenson intervened. "Nightfall beckons. We'll camp right here. Whatever comes or goes will be noticed."

Assignment Done

Upon early morning's call, Aurie visited Sorenson's tent. He stood outside the tent, waited for Sorenson to summon a greeting.

"Enter."

Aurie reached down, unsnapped the lower three clips, then ducked down, slunk through the coarse cloth covering, then stood erect and awaited the usual multiple requests which needed attention immediately.

"Ah. It is you. Thought you were lost," Sorenson said.

"No. Just trying to maintain order," Aurie said.

"So, I know what you are," Sorenson said.

"Yes, well, such discovery was inevitable for a man such as yourself."

"Don't think you can take from me any more than I have already promised. No additional shares."

"Understood." He turned to leave.

"Wait."

Here came the kicker. He had been discovered, outed as a ghoul, by either Sorenson's intuition, or worse, ripe speculation.

"Check the dig site once more. I know you can find what we, I seek."

"On it."

The sudden silence served as Sorenson's goodbye, but Aurie held him psychologically longer and read between the lines. Sorenson sensed his secret, and Aurie's actual physical and genetic nature had shown itself to Sorenson. So now he was on the "victim" list, again.

He was hired knowingly, by Hermann Sorenson, to be observed, and for future use as scientific discovery. A ghoul known literally in the earth world. History developed. Exploits chronicled, as grisly as they had become. He would become an experimental tool for Hermann until Hermann was ready to either announce his discovery or use it further to produce results for specific experimental endeavors, which ever profited Hermann more.

Aurie had to ask.

"And what was the point of this endeavor again?"

"To find what is not and determine if it is."

"What is not, is."

"Yes. Well, it's the moment of truth. What are you going to say in the moment of truth."

Aurie thought for a second, although he didn't need to. He just wanted to see one more bead of sweat slow drip from Sorenson's brow, like the last trickle of life from a near exhausted stream bed. He then responded.

"As your tour guide, I suggest we enter the cavern and find the prize."

Sorenson smirked, but his tongue seemed tied to a mildewed mooring post.

"Overconfident and ill-prepared, for this moment," Aurie audibly observed.

"I'm not nervous."

"Rattled."

"Lead the way," Sorenson stated, then picked up a back pack and slung it over his shoulder.

Now the remaining team members had awakened, caught halfway through morning routine.

"They'll catch up," Sorenson said.

Aurie led him to a spot just beyond the point where the team stopped the evening previous. He pushed on a soft spot of the outer cavern wall, it gently retracted until a passable opening appeared. They entered the cavern.

"Already lit, inside, I see," Sorenson said.

"We're not the first," Aurie said.

"Three pairs of eyes in this cavern," Sorenson intoned in a disciplinary manner as a touché attempt.

"Four," Aurie parried back.

"And the worm turns," Sorenson sounded in a nervous cackled voice.

"Yes. I'm the Seventh," Aurie admitted. "You said earlier you knew what I am."

Sorenson blinked.

"I don't believe in the Ratica mythos."

"Still, it is here. In me."

"You are the one? I mean the seventh?"

"And the one is also with me," Aurie added, "and with me is another."

"Awkward bluff, I must say," Sorenson remarked in a confident tone, then asked, "Do you like this male specimen of mine?"

More light beamed from deeper parts of the dank cavern

to allow further intellectual enlightenment. A tall being, covered in whitish brown long hair, stood statue-like, in the shadows.

"This fellow isn't a pet," Aurie advised. "This fellow isn't even a fellow." He winked at her. "She is also a Seventh Ratica."

Sorenson finally unleashed his morality speech and the genesis of his purpose.

"How do you control an entire population? You make them fear everything. Every single thing, from climate change weather anomalies of no significance exaggerated as forceful energies capable of producing end of times potential. From threat of nuclear annihilation to grisly suffocation by virus infection. There are truly Genghis Khan's and worse in this world, bent on absolute control of all around them.'

'And who spreads these viruses of mind diseases. The politicians, their media allies, the propaganda ministers otherwise known as Hollywood., and the final monstrosity of evil in the form of brainwashing, otherwise known as education from the earliest of age to the eldest. Combine all of these tactical mentality control measures, and weapons of war become mere pebbles on the beach.'

'Humanoid slaves are still needed to make the gears of technology grind along, so destruction of all physical beings doesn't serve the underlying purpose of the controllers who are ever-present in the financial markets and technology communications industry. A weapon which fits in the palm of every human hand, first marketed as a convenience entertainment novelty, has been converted into a tracking system integrated into every avenue of population integration. This hypnotic device is called a mobile phone. It has been evolved into a tactical weapon to spy upon all humanoid beings no matter where they stand, sit, or shit. It is now the ground floor of control in a system of evil incarnate, a Hitlerian system still evolving to the nth power. The controller's biggest fear is loss of control."

Aurie took his own vocalization turn.

"I know your world. It's a crazy woke place. In my world, we would have already ripped off the faces of our leaders and fried them up for breakfast."

Sorenson continued, unmoved.

"Just you and I and the beast. The beast is mine now."

"Some of the team is still alive, and I, and you," Aurie said, and added, "I killed some of them, because like you, they came here for profit at the expense of another species."

Sorenson added more sauce to the word meal.

"Balderdash. The beast killed them while under my power of suggestion."

"Did you witness these killings?" Aurie asked.

Sorenson seemed a bit stunned. "Their tracking devices deactivated which could only happen upon death."

"No. I saved some of the team, the ones you brought only as bait in your scheme," Aurie said.

"You jest."

"Are you sure? By the way, it's breakfast time. Turn around."

Sorenson turned and saw the beast who unbeknownst to him had crept up behind, looking back at him, like a mirror image in eye contrast. The beast looked directly into Sorenson's eyes, not as food, but as sentient equals. Yet, hunger intervened as urge in the belly of the beast, so nose twitches and sniff sounds drained wet from beast's face salacious.

"She likes you," Aurie said.

"Not possible," Sorenson toned out, nervously.

"As a meal, maybe more," Aurie continued. "The survivors of our team are here, housed in the cave recesses, under the protection of my friend you call the beast. The others who posed obstacles to my mission completion, or who attempted to sabotage the mission, or who served my necessary nutritional needs are forever gone from this world."

"I don't believe you," Sorenson screamed. "I'm in charge of this group. They will do as I say."

"Unfortunately, not so. You are now prey of the beast, the one you came to enslave. Perhaps she will let you live to serve her needs, until a mate finds a way to her."

Sorenson looked quite steamed. Searched for words, but none boiled forth. Aurie continued explanations.

"The mating system is a bit rugged. Varied Antillean dances, 15 in all. Sometimes the rigors exhaust the male, then the female has her way, to the death. You found what you came for. Enjoy."

"Wait," Sorenson begged. "You can't leave or leave me here. You won't be paid."

"Seriously? Okay. Let's add this moment up by counting past moments. The beast, as you call her, is kin to a Clan from my home world. But her Clan was banished 8 generations ago in our time plan. We call each generation a Ratica.

"I know what you mean by Ratica," Sorenson said.

"Good. The history of each generation builds onto the next. After seven Raticas, the weakest or least productive of the Clans is banished. Must find a new home world. The beast's Clan and my family Clan were friendly and beneficent towards each other for eons, but politics put each of our Clans at the bottom of the essentials list. The beast's Clan agreed to leave, so my Clan, as appreciation, sends ambassadors to the off worlds where they've relocated to help assure species survival."

Sorenson again interceded.

"You don't understand. Alone these creatures are no threat to any species. But together, united, their collective instincts and ferocity of instinct endless makes them the most powerful force in the universe."

Aurie thought for a bit.

"Perhaps they were expelled for that very reason. Fear of their power. They've never exhibited a collective domination tendency, but the powerful of mind, the societal Elites in every culture would automatically consider them a threat, an enemy, to be tamed and used for selfish purposes, as slaves to the Elites."

The creature approached Sorenson, stood a foot above Sorenson's frame, face to face. As the creature bowed its head towards the top of Sorenson's head, it opened its mouth wide and snorted the hair right out from Sorenson's scalp, sprayed blood, and skin upward like an erupted volcano. Sorenson began to collapse, only to be caught in the clutches of the beasts thick, white, hairy arms. The hairs were so taught, in orgasmic and evolutionary joy, they pierced Sorenson's clothing. Blood oozed forth from it, blotted it all the way through the thick winter clothing.

During the process, Sorenson's backpack exploded open
and out rolled two gems he had apparently pilfered from the tundra.

"I trust you will return these," Aurie said as he retrieved them and returned each to the beast.

After Sorenson's demise, Aurie asked his ghoul friend the snow beast where are the others.

They were all comfortable, the few humanoids that remained, hidden in the back cave. The beast clan's target was only the one, Sorenson, as his efforts would have exposed more ghouls to banishment or death, each temporary in effect amongst the ghoul world inhabitants, but still a punishment for transgressions committed on humanoid worlds. The ghouls had survival interests to protect; a necessary purpose in order to continue a watch upon humanoid world machinations, particularly those potentially endangering continued ghoul Clan existence.

One of the remaining male companions of the Team, not yet dead, remarked "I don't know what it is, but it isn't from around this part of the solar system."

"I think you're next on the menu," Aurie responded.

"Do me, you. It couldn't be worse than that thing. And I'd rather not slowly turn into an ice cube, or become ravaged in ritual to death."

"I don't know. My method isn't much different."

"Please, I beg of you."

"Okay, this may hurt a bit."

"Anything but that", the humanoid male pleaded. "It won't last as long, will it?"

"I'll do my best."

Aurie moved over towards him. The male, whose name Aurie had forgotten at this moment, was a bit small in height.

"Open your mouth." His prey obeyed.

"I'll tranquilize you first." Aurie's true physical form started to break through his own humanoid skin cloth and expose a truer physical form as ghoul, taller in height, wider in breadth, then touched his salivating lips to the prey's lips, then quickly and deeply inhaled. His prey shuddered in each limb, flailed a bit, then went limp, but Aurie continued to inhale. The prey's body then began to turn inside out. Aurie hadn't eaten in weeks. The sweet succor of his prey's fluids became intoxicating. "That was real," he said to himself.

The beast prey grunted, groaned. Aurie raised his hand, his back still exposed to the beast. Then completed in his meal consumption, Aurie returned to humanoid form and addressed the beast.

"Sorry big gal. My first meal in a good while. I hope you understand."

A disheartened look and another grunt, then shrug from the beast served as response. Aurie walked away from the scene slowly as the beast collected the remains of this prey, rolled it up in a human flesh ball, then carted what remained of his future meal on each hefty shoulder, to the back of the cave and into darkness. It was over.

Aurie turned and said, "I trust you'll help the survivors on a return to the nearest humanoid occupied location." The beast grunted an approval response.

Aurie wanted to say, "I'll be back some day, to check on you," as a humanoid side of him had begun to accumulate in the psyche over the course of his long existence years, but such niceties were not frequent cultural inclinations amongst his kind. Another ambassador would likely be sent in the future.

He found a wind current, transformed completely into ghoul form, and drifted upward. Not before a long time had passed, a wind current sufficient in velocity blew him forth towards his ultimate destination point. The ghouls had existed long before hominids, had tracked the earth wind currents like terrestrial road map designs. He knew the paths, intersections, entry and exit points. Ecological music radiated in these paths, easy to follow, like modern day radio tunes.

The creature below, in native tongue, howled victory. Then another creature did same, and still another sounded out, along this travel path, over expanses of hundreds of miles until Aurie had cleared the boundaries of the current creature Clan earth-bounded domain.

Aurie's destination resided amidst and among these air current waves, as emanated songs. Songs of ancient times, when a strong yet delicate hand or avian beak swung one thin twig against one thick tree trunk, or hollowed log, or half-sipped coconut, or scraped along a crisp rock surface, or dipped into calm pond waters.

Nature's sounds, plucked by creatures avian active in early morning and insects prone to strum at night, chirped and chattered in their special manner as instructors, eons' seasoned teachers of managed sounds. He followed the music towards earned solace and the find of home.

Lasting Fasting

Aurie finally arrived back home. Found himself in the apartment, the in between travel moments faded like dust in the wind.. His mouse and roach friend were sleeping in the accustomed places, one on the wall above the couch, the other along the couch cloth arm opening, burrowed in the warmth therein. And too, was she, his research assistant, spread out along her back and pressed deep into and amidst the couch pillows. He wondered if she had waited for him, coming over to visit and find only emptiness except for his little friends.

A sudden pang of angst attacked him inside the chest cavity. He didn't quite understand or expect it, yet it was there, and he couldn't shake it. He wanted to shake and wanted not to also. "Look outside, through the window, for to capture a philosophical moment," he thought. Post mission exhaustion had infected him. Resolution of the anxiety eluded him still. Then a whisper captured his ears as gentle syllable hears.

"Hey." Her voice soothed his mind. He imagined, too, it would have soothed his soul, if he still possessed one, yet in dreams he could remember the feeling, of a soul.

"Come here."

Her soft voice tone pounded into his chest cavity, from inside outward. He froze in motion, almost planted solid in form, as his feet acted like anxious iron anchors just dropped into a ravaging ocean current.

He lifted each foot, strained at the thigh, and his muscles tightened firm. He could hear his own breath, feel blow back into his nasal cavity, along his cheeks, across his eyes and brows. Droplets of sweat baptized his forehead creases. He wondered just what had happened. Her voice, her aroma, the sweet and succulent scent had become hypnotic, paralyzing.

He carried his natural shoulder hunch along, and she didn't criticize the appearance of it. A comfort began to blanket him. One more plank on the bridge successfully invaded and traversed. Only a few more to go, and then into her outstretched arms his memories would disappear, for moments that begged eternal. His pounding heart sounds almost obliterated the natural sounds around him; the creak in the floor, the metal screen clicks, wind aided. Her body warmth penetrated his shirt, enveloped around his skin.

"I remember this moment," he thought. He realized it had occurred in him, about him, around him, at least five or six times previous during existence time. A memory spotted of deep and dark holes, empty in appearance, but full of past victories and transgressions, sometimes arose like the cream of a good and hot coffee, while still remained in the cup or mug. The taste of it singed his tongue, then receded into the more exotic revelation portions of the oral digit, until a sentient complacence aroused, massaged his mind, at least into a moment of pleasure clean.

"Self-deception resided in the intellectual ruins of all humankind," he thought. There was nothing more to pretend. And such a thought justified this moment, for the journalist. The busy mind never slept, although the body may have done so.

"Now, back to that question," Aurie said.

"What?"

"Who kissed you and gave you mono in the third grade?"

"Funny. Humanoid talk. Funny," she said.

He began an uncontrollable laugh.

"I stole it from the TV," Aurie admitted.

"You know, this moment has all the earwigs of a kind of pretty good relationship," she said.

"Almost forever has a familiar ring to it. Have to add that action to my 'To Don't Do' list."

Always a price to pay for indiscretion moments. Only question, worth it or not? Temptation twists like a sun's ray sting shot at the ground worm's peek. One can only hope, then act, and maybe the best happens, or at least the better part of best. Or the highest part of worst.

Now his ached belly stormed trombone loud and chill. "Well, the worst is over," he thought, "but the wurst is yet to come." Enter, mind enema. The planet doesn't give a damn about you or me. It would murder us in a heartbeat. Interesting thing about nature. It doesn't give a damn what you think.

Here Lays A Death

In my clan society, earth would be described as occupied by a civilization intent upon destroying itself. We refer to it as a method abhorrent to a harmonious and sustainable continued survival path.

Off earth worlds study earth for lesson planning as means to imprint the message upon citizens of how not to exist in harmony. It is the only reason earth has relevance, still survives in the dimension realms. Lessons for how to fail uplift; support learnings on how to pursue knowledge of the pitfalls inherent along a survival path. Earth still exists despite failures. Epiphanies of mental acuity result.

We are built by our early days, through family, events, triumphs and failures. Our clan history developed from such experiences, helped to forge the path onward, as time demanded such sacrifices. A tipping point occurred in the existence model when present moments became weighed down heavy by volumes of past events whether concluded or completed.

Past then became cherished or scorned. Present evolved into more mellowed memory than concrete events. Our youth faded, passed on to another fresher youth, our progeny. Their present becomes prologue to our future final story. Machinations broken, repaired, retooled. The stars have yet to burn away.

"I remember you."

The Ghoulish End
Books by Mike Gutowski:

Cratch
Time for the Dead: Zombies-A Love Story
Ariadne
Misfortunes Of Mister Knack
available on Amazon.com

"Viewers or imbibers of art works set upon a discovery journey into the place where destination can only become prescient in them alone." --
The Author

www.ingramcontent.com/pod-product-compliance
Lightning Source LLC
Chambersburg PA
CBHW070402200726
48294CB00003B/1054